ACCEPT NO ATTITUDE

ACCEPT NO ATTITUDE

P.I.V.O.T. LAB CHRONICLES™ BOOK FOUR

MICHAEL ANDERLE

LMBPN Publishing
PMB 196, 2540 South Maryland Pkwy
Las Vegas, NV 89109

First US Edition, December, 2020
(Previously published as a part of *Choosing What Matters*)
eBook ISBN: 978-1-64971-346-9
Print ISBN: 978-1-64971-347-6

Jacob tapped his foot as he read. Although late at night, he wasn't tired. Lately, no longer drained by the constant worry about PIVOT going under for financial reasons or their first test subject dying in the game, he felt like he was walking on air.

When he and his friends had developed their virtual reality system years before, he had known it was a feat of engineering. He had loved losing himself in the days and nights of testing and problem-solving. They had all known that PIVOT was extremely ambitious as a project but had exceeded even their wildest dreams.

Still, something had been missing.

Like the rest of his team, he had chosen to work in engineering to change the world. No matter how complex the problems he was solving with the virtual reality pods were, he wasn't entirely happy merely making an entertainment system.

Everything had changed in an instant when Amber, one of his two co-founders, realized that the pods could be repurposed to provide medical care to coma patients. The team had then stumbled upon research showing that virtual reality could be used to help comatose patients recover more quickly.

The road from there to here had been anything but smooth. They had faced financial ruin, media harassment, and even jail time. However, their first patient had woken from his coma and was in recovery, PIVOT had been acquired and funded extensively, and the three founding members were now inundated with the kind of work they'd craved for the better part of a decade.

As a result, he wasn't sad about the late nights and in fact, he reveled in them.

"You're enjoying that K-pop, huh?" Nick asked.

"Huh?" Jacob looked up and took a moment to listen. At some point, the music they were playing had changed from rock to bouncy Korean pop with half-English choruses and synthy undercurrents. With a small frown, he tried to decide whether to care, gave up, bopped his head in a chair dance, and returned to his work.

Amber gave the other man a thumbs-up. "I told you he wouldn't mind."

Nick nodded. He was chair-dancing in time with Jacob. "I'll hate you for getting us into this, won't I?"

"No." She gave a seated shimmy and spun her chair. "Because there's so much of it and it's all happy and danceable."

"What did you say it was?" Jacob asked.

"It's K-pop," she explained. "First, you think it's a little cheesy, then you find one or two catchy songs, and a month later, it's all you've listened to." She gave an exaggerated shrug and took a bite of cold pizza. "God, I'm *so hungry*. Why am I so hungry?"

"I don't know, but I am too." He shook his mouse to wake his computer up. "Wait, yes I do. Guys, it's four thirty."

"No," she protested, "because we ordered the pizza at six."

"Yeah." Jacob gave her a meaningful nod. "I meant it's four thirty *AM*."

"What?" Amber picked her phone up and stabbed the power button a few times. "Well, my phone is dead so I can't check. I think we should probably get some rest."

"Yeah." Jacob yawned. "Now that I think about it, I'm very tired."

"Let's get breakfast," Nick suggested.

"Will anything be open?"

"It's New York City. Of course something will be open. Come on." He stood and shrugged his coat on.

"I did finish an application, I guess." Jacob started tidying up. The applications, which contained numerous sections of medical information, all had to be locked in cabinets. He stacked the ones he had completed and placed them in one pile, then made another of unread ones beside it.

He'd worked for almost twenty-four hours straight and the unread pile was still twice as high as the reviewed pile. A glance showed that his partners were in a similar situation, and he knew they had only printed out the first quarter of what they had received thus far.

They passed through the two layers of security necessary to leave the Diatek Offices and emerged a little wearily into the very first part of dawn. Even at this hour, New York bustled with a relatively even blend of people in suits, those in various cleaning or fast food uniforms, and others who looked like they had no reason to be awake at all.

Amber shivered in the cold. "I forgot how much I hate New England winters."

"Do me a favor," Nick said, "and don't call New York 'New England' where anyone can overhear us. I don't want to get beaten to within an inch of my life."

"It's too cold to make promises," she said desolately. "Hey, that place looks open."

"Do you even know what blintzes are?"

"It says there's cheese, and there's a sign with a coffee cup. That's good enough for me."

They entered the little two-table restaurant, where the chef didn't greet them but bellowed into the back of the shop about customers. The waitress appeared a few moments later, still smelling of cigarette smoke but with three cups of surprisingly strong coffee.

"Breakfast special?" she asked. In the complete absence of any response, she nodded again and bawled their order into the kitchen as she disappeared—presumably to finish her cigarette.

"I wonder what we'll get," Jacob said.

"It's a mystery," Amber said prosaically. "So? Did anyone have interesting applications?"

"Not really." He shook his head. "Honestly, the real issue will be trying to sort through all the younger guys who want to go in. I get unreasonably excited whenever I see one that isn't a guy in his twenties or thirties."

"I've had a few," Nick said. "A fair number have weird health problems—the kind of things where doctors don't know why."

"That's almost all of mine," she said. "Things doctors can't seem to fix or diagnose or whatever. I have no idea how some of them think we can help them, but I guess they're looking for anything at this point."

"I'm not looking forward to writing a response to all of them," Jacob said with a groan.

"This is what form letters were invented for," Nick told him.

"I can't send a form letter to people who are desperate for help. But I...we need more baseline patients before we can even start branching out."

"We'll come up with something," she told him. "Don't worry. We can even explain a version of that, right?"

The cook banged on the bell and slid three plates up. When no one came to take them, he banged on it again, came out of the kitchen in a filthy apron while muttering about bad service, and brought them the plates himself. He banged them on the table and left out the back door, where a storm of yelling erupted in a language that might or might not have been English.

"So, these are blintzes, huh?" Amber poked one with her fork. "Well, let's give this a try. Cheers."

Dorothy sipped her coffee and stared out the window, and she turned when a knock sounded on the door.

The first was restrained. The second was a wild pounding, half-knuckles and half-flat hands, and it was accompanied by shouting. "Great-grandma! Great-grandma! Great-grandma!"

With a smile, she moved to the door. She didn't walk quite fast enough to satisfy her great-grandson, but she knew Liam merely wanted to imitate the grown-ups by knocking. Experience made her careful and she opened the door a crack so he wouldn't spill into the house, then pulled it open when he had righted himself.

"Great-grandma!" Liam tumbled inside and threw his arms around her legs. "Pick me up!"

"Hello." She rested one faintly trembling hand on his reddish-brown head. "I can't pick you up, pumpkin. You're getting too big for that."

His pout was fleeting. He was distracted quickly enough by the thought of Great-grandma's house and raced into the living room.

"Careful!" she called after him. "And take your shoes off!" Mary, Dorothy's daughter-in-law, shook her head with a rueful laugh and bent to give her a hug. Tall and willowy, with blonde hair she had begun to let go gray, the younger woman looked her usual, put-together self. She held some banana bread out. "We have Liam today and I thought we could drop this off before going to the park. Sorry it's so early."

"What do you think I get up to?" Dorothy asked. She gestured at the empty house. "I've been up for a few hours now anyway. We can have coffee if you want while Liam plays."

"That sounds lovely." Mary followed her inside. "John mentioned you weren't sleeping well lately."

"Old bones." She shrugged. "This hip hasn't felt right for a while now. As my grandma used to say, 'don't get old.'"

The other woman laughed ruefully as she sat at the table and waited for the coffee. Unlike her husband, she didn't rush to do everything for her mother-in-law. It was a small gesture but one Dorothy appreciated—she didn't like being treated like an invalid.

Mary sat quietly while she brought the sugar and cream, pausing frequently as Liam dashed through the kitchen with various toys. With nine great-grandchildren, Dorothy had acquired a pile of toys that had been forgotten at her house over the years.

When the old woman at last came to sit, Mary clinked her mug against hers with a smile. "Should I cut the banana bread?"

"Of course." Dorothy watched as a thick slice came away from the loaf, studded with chocolate chips. "I can't wait. Did Liam help you make it?"

"For certain definitions of the word 'help.'" Mary smiled. "He put in about twice as many chocolate chips as the recipe called for. I'm surprised it's holding together at all." She passed her a plate.

"Mmm, thank you." Her mother-in-law took a bite and tried not to let her face fall too obviously. The woman was a wonderful baker and the bread was almost certainly delicious, but lately, Dorothy hadn't been able to taste much of everything. Her mouth always seemed to taste of metal. To avoid being rude, she took another bite. "It's as good as always."

"Thank you." Mary took a slice for herself. "What are you up to today?"

She smiled. "Not much of anything. As per usual."

"You could come to the park with us," her companion suggested.

"Ah, thank you, but no. I have a doctor's appointment at eleven." She saw Mary's quick look. "It's only routine."

"Well, be sure to mention the sleeping," the woman advised her.

"Now you sound like my son."

"No, if I were John, I would tell you to go out and have a date tonight." Mary gave her a conspiratorial smile before she rolled her eyes.

"He does keep talking about that." Dorothy sighed. "Most children aren't so keen to replace their father."

"He's sixty-two," Mary pointed out with a laugh. "It's not like he's in much need of fatherly guidance." She paused before she said gently, "And it has been ten years."

Her sigh was a little heavier this time.

"I'm not trying to rush you," the younger woman said hurriedly. "I only want to make sure you aren't...well—Liam, please don't throw books. Oh, what was I saying?" She frowned.

"Look who's getting old now," Dorothy teased. She shook her head. "I'm not lonely, Mary. I don't need a husband."

"I know you don't." Mary wrapped her fingers around her mug of coffee. "And I do tell John that whenever he mentions it. It's only..."

She raised an eyebrow in the best imitation she could muster of her grandmother. That woman had been the undisputed champion of withering stares.

Apparently, hers weren't as frightening, because her daughter-in-law merely smiled a little sadly. She clasped Dorothy's hand for a moment. "I feel like there's something missing from your life," she said. "Not necessarily a husband. But you don't have friends you spend time with either, Dotty. You've always seemed like the kind of person to me who..."

Dorothy frowned. "Was a recluse?"

"No, no, that's not what I mean at all." Mary chewed a piece of banana bread as she tried to find the words. "I always expect you to say you've taken up sculpting or writing novels. You seem like someone who's so passionate about the world." She smiled and took a sip of her coffee. "Maybe you simply never tell us about your interests."

"I…" She took a moment to process that. To be polite, she took another bite of the banana bread, even though all she could taste was metal. "I've never had any particular hobbies. Now it's a little too late, don't you think? What would I do? Play shuffleboard? Go out and look at the sea?"

"Whatever you *want*." The younger woman stood and kissed her cheek. "Right now, though, you need to get to your doctor's appointment, so Liam and I will get out of your hair."

"Mmm." Dorothy pushed from the table with a wince. "Thank you for bringing the banana bread."

"Eat a few more slices," Mary advised. "You've been losing weight. Are you sure you feel okay?"

"Yes," she assured her and rolled her eyes. "Goodbye, Liam."

"Bye, Great-grandma!" The door slammed.

"I should go get him," Mary said, alarmed. She darted to the door. "Come have dinner tonight!"

"I…well, I'm not sure I—"

"Six thirty?" Mary slipped her shoes on hurriedly. "John would love to see you and James will be over to pick Liam up. Say you will?"

Before she could answer, Mary had left, calling for Liam to not run into the street.

Dorothy sighed. It appeared she would go to dinner, which was only a problem because she wasn't looking forward to eating another metal-tasting meal. Mary was right, though. She *had* been losing weight. It was preferable to not eat much compared to eating more mouthfuls of chicken that tasted like tin.

With another sigh, she went to get her coat. She should leave for the doctor's office. It was early but it wasn't like she had much else to do.

It was funny, what Mary had said about her interests. Dorothy had never had any hobbies. There hadn't been time and now, as she'd said, there wasn't much of a point.

That made her feel sad, and she shook her head as she stepped into the sunlight. It wasn't like she'd had a bad life. She had a lovely family, she'd adored her husband, and she lived comfortably now. Things could be much worse.

She merely felt a little numb.

Even an hour later, as Dorothy stood distractedly in the doctor's reception room with charts and scans clutched in one trembling hand, the numbness didn't lift. A metal taste in her mouth, an aching hip, the low energy, and the sleeplessness—all the little things she associated with growing older—weren't little at all.

She looked at the scans again and couldn't find anything to feel except resignation.

"You've done it now, Dotty," she told herself. It was what her mother always used to say when she messed up.

For a moment, she'd thought seriously about sculpting or writing. Mary was right, the world was full of interesting things.

There merely wasn't much point when you were eighty-four and you had cancer.

CHAPTER TWO

The thing she was most frightened of, Dorothy realized, was that her family would find out and they would be upset. She didn't think she could deal with them fussing over her. During the entire ride home from the doctor's office, she tried to think of lies to tell them or ways to share the truth so they wouldn't worry.

In the end, she decided not to say anything at all—although she did stop at a local bakery to buy kugel, which she knew was James's favorite. It had been a long time since she did anything like that, but she didn't have to be quite as careful with money now, she reasoned.

She arrived to the usual chaos of Liam, who wrestled with James on the living room rug while John looked on indulgently from his favorite chair. Mary's son came to give her a hug and take the kugel.

"You look tired," he told her.

"Don't you start." Her voice was a little sharper than normal. "If the doctor isn't worried, you shouldn't be either."

Huh. Apparently, she had decided to lie. That was interesting.

"So you did speak to him." John looked relieved, although that was probably because he didn't have to come up with a creative way to pry the truth out of her without seeming to ask. "Mary said you told her you would."

"You two need to come up with more exciting things to discuss," Dorothy told him as fondly as she could. "Your father and I didn't have fifty happy years by talking about other people's health, I'll tell you that."

John, who was used to her ribbing, only smiled. He and Mary were coming up on thirty years of marriage and they quite clearly adored each other as much as they had when they got married. They were the ones she never needed to worry about, for which she was grateful. Deborah was still angry about the divorce, even all these years later, and Deborah and her husband didn't seem all that happy.

Robert, the youngest and an avowed bachelor, was one Dorothy worried about more out of form than anything else. Since she'd been widowed, she'd developed an appreciation for her son's independence, and the two of them had grown closer than she had expected. She still gave him grief about finding a nice woman to settle down with and he still rolled his eyes, but it was firmly an act now. After all, she heard the same lines from the other children.

Mary greeted her with a kiss on the cheek and a glass of wine.

"Oh, no thank you," Dorothy protested.

"I would," the woman advised. "John cooked."

She took the glass of wine with John's protests in the background.

"He did well." James appeared in the doorway with Liam hanging over one shoulder. "I taught him how to make roast pork."

"Will wonders never cease?" Dorothy managed a smile. "I'll reserve judgment until I've had some, I think."

"Fair." John put oven mitts on with a flourish. "But you'll eat your words. James is an excellent teacher."

James smiled with smug satisfaction. After selling a business, he'd been at loose ends lately. Even though he had enough money to never work again and his wife earned a great deal of money as a corporate lawyer, he was never content doing nothing. In the past four months, Dorothy had heard talk of a PhD, a cookbook, a sailboat, and several more companies.

She considered him as the family sat down to a dinner that was, admittedly, excellent. Like her, he had done everything that was expected of him in life. He'd gotten married, had a child, and run a successful business. That wasn't enough for him, though. He had dozens of other interests—almost, she could say, he found everything interesting.

Did Mary honestly think Dorothy was the same?

With a start, she realized someone had asked her something. She looked around in surprise.

"Mom, are you okay?" John looked worried.

"Oh, don't you start again," she said. "I was daydreaming, that's all. What were you talking about?"

"I hoped you would talk your grandson out of trying to build a boat," he said. "As it seems neither I nor his wife can persuade him."

"I *want* Dada to build a boat!" Liam said excitedly.

"See?" James said with a serene smile. "Liam's vote is most important."

"I don't see why he shouldn't build a boat," she weighed in.

Everyone gave her an incredulous look—except Liam, who cheered from his seat.

"You're in favor of this?" John asked. "He won't be able to sail a wooden boat around here."

"Maybe I'll simply sell it," the other man said.

"You'll get attached to it," Mary predicted fondly, "and you'll need to rent a storage unit to keep it in because you can't bear to give it up, but you'll never have time to sail it."

James grumbled.

"If you want to build a boat, you build a boat," Dorothy said. "Don't you listen to them. You have many interests and you always have. Maybe you'll find your next business while building it."

He lifted his glass to her in a toast. "Grandma's on board *and* Liam's on board."

"Don't you dare take either of them on a boat before it's been tested," Mary said with mock severity. "And then only with several life-jackets."

Dorothy sat in the living room and listened as they all cleaned up and bickered good-naturedly about the boat. Building one didn't sound at all interesting to her because she'd been born in the era where people did things like that because they had to, not because it was a fun diversion. Still, she admired James for being so passionate.

"Dotty?" Mary returned with the bottle of wine. "Would you like any more?" She frowned at the look on her mother-in-law's face. "Are you sure you're all right? I won't tell John if you aren't, I promise."

She summoned a smile from somewhere. "I'm fine. Merely tired. The doctor prescribed something."

Chemotherapy was what the doctor had prescribed.

And while she might not be sure what she wanted to do in life, she knew she didn't particularly want to be even sicker than she was. The thought of something like chemotherapy filled her with dread.

And that was what her family wouldn't understand. They would want her to recover and get better.

But why? Dorothy didn't want to spend her last years in pain and sick to her stomach. She wanted....well, she didn't know what she wanted. That was the problem.

The two men were still bickering when they entered the living room, and it took Dorothy a few moments to realize the subject had changed.

"Like I'll trust a senator to tell me about healthcare," John said with a snort.

She looked at Mary for clarification, only for her daughter-in-law to shake her head and shrug. "I don't understand it either. I thought virtual reality was headsets."

"Some of it is," James said patiently. "Liam, don't run with the hot chocolate. Sit at the table to drink it." He went to help the boy with his drink before he returned to the living room with a beer in hand. "This is a full neural hookup. You don't put it over your eyes and see a screen. It tells your optic nerves what you're seeing."

"That's even worse," John said. "I don't want them to put things in my brain."

"Many technologies we accept now were things that seemed unreasonable at the time," the other man said. "Look, it's getting FDA approval and they're searching for test subjects. I think it would be fun. I'd like my next project to do something similar."

"I don't get it." Dorothy felt the usual prickliness she experienced when talking about technology. "Is it for blind people?"

"It could be," he said thoughtfully. "That's part of what they're testing now—they want to know how different people use it. It's in the news because it helped a senator's son out of his coma."

"*Maybe*," John said darkly. "People wake up from comas all the time."

"And often, they don't," James said, still patient but with a trace of steel in his voice. "It could be an interesting treatment and it's always good to have new ones. It's not like we have comas fully explained. Besides, the game simply sounds fun."

"There's a game?" She was completely confused now.

"Yeah. Like World of Warcraft or—okay, you don't know what that is. Hmm, Dungeons and Dragons?"

"That," John said, "was not the way to convince your grandmother. She used to lecture me endlessly about games like that."

"You always had your nose in a book about spaceships or dragons," Dorothy protested. "And such a brilliant mind."

"Grandma." James sounded disappointed but almost as if he had the moral high ground. "Merely because someone likes science fiction and fantasy or video games doesn't mean they're wasting their talents. Some science fiction stories are the most illuminating, most—" He shook his head as he searched for words. "And not every book has to be serious. Besides, don't I remember you reading romance novels?"

John crowed with laughter.

"I did," she said stiffly, "but I didn't like them much."

"I wouldn't judge you if you had," James said, with a laugh. "I'm only saying that people like different things. And if you do still read romance novels, Mom always has a stack of them."

Mary settled into her seat with a stern look at her husband. "Not a word out of you. And if your mother always got on your case for what you read, why would you get on mine for my romance novels?"

"That's a good point," he admitted. He gave his mother a wicked grin. "And I admit, I did play Dungeons and Dragons a few times."

"What!" She could not imagine her straight-laced son, the executive, playing trite games about dragons and wizards. "*Why?*"

"Why don't you play?" James asked and cut his father's intended response off, "and then maybe you'd know? Any number of people play D&D with their grandparents. We could make it a weekly thing." His raised eyebrow said he knew she wouldn't say yes, then he laughed: "Or you could go into the virtual reality game. I bet if you were a wizard slinging fireballs, you'd find that very cool."

Dorothy snorted.

"Shake your head all you want," he said, "but I'll believe until proven otherwise that you would like to throw spells and wield a sword."

"Your grandmother," John told his son severely, "would be much more of a crossbow woman."

Mary burst out laughing and Dorothy, despite her innate resistance to the idea, chuckled. What would they say, she wondered, if she did start playing those games?

The question reminded her of the topic she had come to avoid, and she swallowed slightly. Fireballs and dragons and swords weren't her thing.

Or were they? Now that she thought about it, she remembered that once or twice, she had stopped in the hallway to read a few pages of the novels she'd taken from John. She had always shaken her head at the dramatic plot twists and strange names but could admit that they'd held some appeal.

She'd always spent time wondering about what came next. In fact, after a while, she'd taken to skipping to the end of the book so she didn't have to wonder. It would be interesting to see if it was too late to track some of those down now.

When she left later that evening, she kissed James on the cheek. "What were you talking about? The thing that shows you stories in your brain."

"Oh, the company is called PIVOT." He pulled his phone out. "I'll text you the information. It was good to see you, Grandma. I'm sorry Liam won't sit still these days."

"He's little," she said with a smile. "Little ones are like that." She didn't add that he was, in a way, the easiest one to be around right now because she didn't feel the need to hide anything from him.

The rest of them presented her with her greatest challenge.

What would she tell them? She had no idea.

CHAPTER THREE

From the first pictures she saw of the PIVOT game, Dorothy knew it was not for her.

The fourteen additional pages of artwork she looked at only cemented that, but to make sure, she decided to watch all of what was apparently called "gameplay videos." She rolled her eyes at the videos of a character confronting his evil twin, scoffed loudly when a dragon appeared on-screen and shook her head when she saw the giant coliseum.

The game was nothing but a mish-mash of power fantasies. Of course, it would be fun to be able to throw fireballs like one character did or ride a dragon, but the real world didn't involve those things. That was why it was important to—

Dorothy stopped that line of thought abruptly and reconsidered.

Most books, even classics, were works of fiction.

She chewed over that thought and made herself another cup of tea before she sat to watch an interview with Justin Williams, the first patient to have recovered using the PIVOT technology. He looked pale and he was still recovering, but he spoke passionately—as did his mother and father—about the effects of the treatment.

What most impressed her was the way his parents spoke about watching their son come into his own by playing the game. With the father in a suit and the mother wearing pearls, they didn't exactly seem like lax, anything-goes parents. Not only that, they had found value not only in their son's recovery but in the things he had learned in the game.

"What does someone learn about real life from riding a dragon?" Dorothy asked no one in particular.

Still, she continued to watch until long after midnight, and when she considered getting up and going to bed, she knew she would merely lie awake, tossing and turning. Instead, she looked up the Dungeons and Dragons games John said he had played and some of the books she could remember. She read book reviews that claimed certain works of speculative fiction were even allegories to current events, although she snorted at that because it was plainly ridiculous.

Then, she kept reading.

Dorothy looked up the PIVOT website and found their application requirements.

She absolutely would not do this.

Still, she *did* have copies of all of her recent health records.

You know, if she intended to do it, which she didn't. She definitely didn't.

There was no point in filling out the whole application, including next of kin. She also most certainly did not need to take the time to write and edit a statement about why she wanted to be in the trial since she didn't want to be part of it.

Thank you for considering my application. I am applying for this trial because I think you will not have many older people applying and you say you need all ages. As you will see from the included records, there is no need to worry about my safety.

For my whole life, I have done what was expected of me. I tried to avoid doing frivolous things. I do not understand how one can find value in playing an artificial game and learning to use magic when that skill cannot be used in the real world. However, I cannot deny that Justin Williams and his family have found great value in your game.

Dorothy continued to scan the letter as her thoughts wavered from one choice to the other. She could not seriously be considering doing this.

Before she could stop herself, she pressed the button to send the application.

The regret was immediate, but no matter how many times she clicked the back button, she could not undo the send of her materials. She opened her email, only to see—with a sinking sensation—a confirmation that she had sent it.

What had she been thinking? They would see her application and laugh at her—an eighty-four-year-old woman who knew nothing about video games. They would want people like James.

Embarrassed, she stood and washed her mug out carefully before she wandered to bed. She knew she wouldn't be able to sleep but she should try. That's what she would have told her children to do when they woke up and said they couldn't sleep. It was the kind of thing she had done her whole life—play by the rules.

Dorothy knew she was fortunate. She'd had a happy marriage, she wasn't in poverty, and she loved her children, grandchildren, and great-grandchildren.

But she'd never had something to feel passionate about. She'd never done anything that was simply for her. Maybe it was only the knowledge that she didn't have much time but right now, that seemed more important than it ever had.

"You know," Jacob said, "you'd think we would have learned from last night to not stay up until all hours."

"Shpf, *learning capabilities.*" Nick waved his hands. "We don't have those."

"Exactly," Amber said. "We're merely three Masters graduates from MIT. What d'you think we have? Life skills? Don't be absurd."

"We're basically contractually obligated to stay up too late and eat too many dehydrated noodles," Nick finished.

Both of them looked at Jacob with identical too-big smiles.

He snickered and returned to work. If he had to wade through this hellscape of paperwork with anyone, he was glad it was the two of them. He sorted the last of his applications into an alphabetized pile and carried them to one of the assistants' desks.

With the benefit of a little sleep and considerably more coffee—as well as a large to-go order of blintzes, which were a new favorite—the team had come up with a form letter that he didn't feel bad about sending. It explained that it would be irresponsible to try to treat diverse medical problems with the pods at this time, but that the applicants' information would be kept on file and they would be contacted for any relevant trials in the future.

"Has anyone heard from Justin?" Nick asked. Their first patient had successfully woken up from his coma a few weeks before and he was now recovering at home in California. He and his parents had offered to be brand ambassadors of a sort.

Not to mention that both Justin and his mother had become a part of the game world.

"Yep." Jacob locked the applications away carefully. "He's doing well and still gaining strength. Being in a coma for three months apparently plays hell with everything from lung capacity to finger muscles. He also reports being unreasonably angry that he can't throw fireballs anymore."

"Ugh," Amber said. "Imagine trying to do physical therapy with an angry wizard. That would be a dangerous job, I tell you." She shook her head. "Any idea when he'll be back, Jacob?"

"He said he can do in-game stuff any time now," he said,

"although Mary then wrote to say the doctor has advised no more than two hours at a time. He still gets tired easily. I talked to DuBois about his data—now that he's not comatose, he interacts with the game in a different way. I didn't understand most of the monologue but I gather we've gained useful data during the couple of times he played."

"Awesome." She put another application in her done pile and frowned at her computer screen. Suddenly focused, she read through something, her head tilted, and finally bit her lip. "Jacob, take a look at the newest one in the shared inbox."

Jacob pushed to roll to his desk and squinted at the screen. "Not a younger dude—score! Oh. *Oh.* Wait, seriously? She's eighty-four?"

"I gotta see this." Nick came to lean over the back of his chair.

Jacob read the details with a frown. He opened the medical files and scanned through them, intrigued by her mention that there was no need to worry about the danger of the experiments.

When he saw what she meant, he put a hand over his mouth.

"She seems interesting," Amber said.

"She's dying," he said.

"Wait—what?" She hurried closer. "She said she wasn't worried about the dangers and I thought that meant—"

"It meant she's already *dying*," Jacob said. "That's why she's not worried. Jesus Christ, we can't put a dying woman into a pod and expect it to go well. Can you imagine the press we'd get if we did that?" He saw his partners exchange a look. "What?"

"She wants to help," Nick said. "And she makes a good point. She's not in good shape, and if she chose between chemotherapy and hospice care, it's not like anyone would blame the hospice workers. Not only that, she's right that we need data from women her age who don't have brain trauma. She's the ideal candidate."

Jacob shook his head emphatically. "Nope. No way. Her body is already under stress and if she dies in the game—which, let's be honest, she'll do if she's eighty-four and hasn't ever played video games in her life—she's at a huge risk of her heart never starting again. Then, we're in the news for killing an old woman."

Amber folded her arms.

"What?" He looked from her to Nick, who also looked deeply unimpressed. "I know none of us studied marketing but come on, you have to admit this doesn't exactly sound like a commercial. Not a successful one, anyway."

"Do you remember what you said about Justin when we started getting all that bad press?" she asked him.

"That it was the right thing to do so the press didn't matter, yes, but this is different."

"Is it?" She held a hand up to forestall his protest. "Yeah, I get it. Justin needed our treatment to survive and she doesn't. But we need baseline data in order to help people her age, she wants to give it to us, and she's giving us a gift. Let's be honest. If we put enough people in the machine who are in their eighties, one of them will eventually die. She's here because she doesn't fear that and she knows something else will kill her sooner or later. In simple terms, she wants her death to mean something. Both from the perspective of the data and the fact that we could make her last months comfortable instead of painful…well, this seems like the right thing to do."

Jacob looked at Nick and was annoyed to see the other man nodding. He leaned back in his chair. "I don't…I don't think I can do it, guys."

His partners looked at one another and seemed to have a silent argument about who would talk to him. Amber lost and moved closer to him and looked him in the eyes.

"Jacob." She tapped him on the knee. "What would your grandmother say?"

"Oh, come *on*." His grandmother had died a few months before, only days before Justin was put into the game. In fact, they had intended that she be the first patient but she had passed away before their treatment could help her.

"The next time that happens to someone," she said, "we'll need the baseline data to help them as well as we can. And you *know* your grandmother wouldn't stand for you coddling an old woman."

Jacob groaned and tipped his head back.

They were right. He hated it when they were right.

"I knew I made a mistake hiring you two," he said.

"*Hiring?*" Amber's voice was dangerous. "We *co-founded* this organization."

Jacob looked up, saw the expression on her face and Nick's, and decided the best he could do now was cut his losses. "Have I mentioned how good you two look these days? Radiant. Shining like…like… Hey, you know what, I'll order us all more blintzes, my treat."

They both folded their arms.

"*Fine.*" He ran a hand through his hair. "I'll call the old lady."

"Good." Amber sat again. "But blintzes first."

CHAPTER FOUR

Justin was lying on the couch and stared vaguely into space when his father came into the room.

"Are you okay?" Tad asked worriedly. Only recently returned from a vote in DC, he hadn't even changed out of his suit yet, although he'd taken the tie and suit jacket off. He held a plate of steamed chicken and vegetables.

"I'm fine," he said with as much patience as he could muster. "But I'm tired all the time. Also, I do not want to eat *any* of that."

"Doctor's orders," his father said. "Protein and vegetables."

"I'm fairly sure I saw the email and it said sushi and cake." He held a hand up. "No, no, think about it. Sushi has vegetables, protein...whatever's in seaweed..."

Tad's mouth twitched. "And what are the nutrients in cake, pray tell?"

"Um. Well, there's carbohydrates. And, uh...brains need glucose! That's it. Glucose. And I think I heard there's something good for you in chocolate."

"Interesting." His dad looked at the sad, wilted meal. "Okay, I'll get you some if you don't tell your mother. But only because this looks horrendous."

A door banged somewhere nearby and he heard his mother's voice and Tina's.

"Don't tell," Tad whispered, and he dumped the vegetables and chicken in a wastebasket and hurried to the kitchen, leaving Justin chuckling behind him.

Not laughing. That still hurt.

He waved tiredly when Tina came into the room. "How are you?"

"Good." She looked suspiciously at the blankets. "You haven't been up and about, have you?"

"Oh, for the love of—will everyone *stop* coddling me?" He glared at her.

"We're not coddling you but trying to help you recover from *being in a coma*." Tina was not cowed in the least by his annoyance. "Which we apparently need to do since you refuse to do anything the doctor recommends."

Justin sighed quietly.

She sat on the side of the couch. "I know it must be hard," she said.

"You think?" He folded his arms. "I was able to go wherever I wanted, shoot fireballs, run around—now, I can't even get across the room without wanting to sit."

"Yes, but last week, you couldn't even get across the room at all," she pointed out. She squeezed his hand. "The reason you could do things like throw fireballs and swing a sword was because you took the time to practice and level up. That's what you're doing now."

"I suppose that's true," he said, slightly mollified. "I have to say, though, leveling up in real life isn't as fun as leveling up in a game."

Tina smiled. She moved around the room and opened windows as he retrieved his phone and looked despondently at it. There were only so many times he could scroll through his social media feeds without becoming deathly bored.

There was a new email, however.

"Holy shit," Justin said. "They want me to come back into the game."

"Oh?" Tina came to kneel at the couch and read over his shoulder. "An eighty-four-year-old woman?" She looked at Justin. "She's gonna get on your case for not putting your pinky out while drinking pints of ale, isn't she?"

He laughed and regretted it when his ribs ached. "Oh, fuck—ow. I don't know, it sounds interesting. If she wants to go into a video game, she must be cool, right? Do you know any grandmas who play VR games?"

She looked dubious but she nodded. "I suppose there's that. Can I go with you?"

"What?" He looked at her. "To help do orientation for this woman?"

"Kinda. I don't know." She shrugged. "I miss the game."

"Really?"

"I never get to stab anyone anymore."

Justin put his head in his hands and tried not to laugh. "I'll ask them. You'd have to come to New York with me."

"That's fine. The less time I spend with my family, the better." Tina shook her head meaningfully. "They're still being crazy about this whole thing."

He slid an arm around her shoulders and although he did it carefully, it still ached. *Everything* ached.

"It's a weird situation," he said.

"You got that right." Tina stood. "Okay, I'll go work on my portfolio for a while. You take a nap. Have you had lunch yet?"

"Uh...yeah." He had heard his father leave and he hoped it was for takeout sushi. "I'll reply to them and then I'll nap. You go work." She had been busy with her art portfolio lately, and her work was not only gorgeous but surprisingly soft and upbeat. He had commented on the profusion of pretty landscapes and flowers, only to be threatened with death if he ever breathed so much as a word about it on social media.

Tina smiled and disappeared and he lay on the couch again.

Introducing new people to the world had appeal. He had to admit, he was happy to return to the game. His recovery went well, all things considered, but there were times when his weakness frustrated him.

He couldn't wait to introduce someone else to it all.

"You're being awfully mysterious," James said to Dorothy.

"You'll understand soon," she told him. She moved down the sidewalk at her top speed, which was still not fast enough for her grandson. "Slow down."

"I want to know where we're going." He hopped from one foot to the other.

"Well, I see now where Liam gets his energy."

"*That* wasn't a mystery." He smiled. "You know, we're very close to Tara's office. Maybe I'll go see her after whatever our mysterious errand is."

Dorothy smiled. She looked at the gleaming skyscraper next to them and picked out the numbers on the side. "This is it. Come on."

Inside, the lobby was an expanse of gleaming marble with a concierge desk, the Diatek logo displayed proudly on the front. Beside it, more recently applied, was another logo.

James stopped dead.

"PIVOT?" he asked her.

"Yes," she said as serenely as she could manage. She approached the desk slowly. "My name is Dorothy Hunt. I'm here to see Jacob Zachary."

"Of course, ma'am," the man at the desk said politely. "And this is?"

"James Hunt. My grandson."

"I'll let Mr. Zachary know you've arrived," the concierge told her.

James drew her away while they waited. "Wait, why are we here? Did you get me into the trial?"

"No." She waited for him to get it and then shook her head. "*I'll* be part of the trial."

"*What?*" He spoke loudly enough that everyone in the lobby looked around. Disconcerted, he leaned closer to whisper, "What? *You?*"

"You needn't sound so surprised." Dorothy drew herself tall, which was difficult these days. "I was interested the other night."

"Grandma, this is…" He looked worriedly at her. "This might be dangerous."

With a start, she realized he would learn about her diagnosis if he accompanied her. She had wanted him to come along because he seemed to know about these things and would be able to help her ask the right questions, but she hadn't thought to prep him.

"Oh, dear," she said worriedly.

"Mrs. Hunt?" a voice asked. A young man not much older than James stood at the security gates.

She fought the urge to turn and flee. At her age, it took a long time to flee. She looked from Jacob Zachary to her grandson and finally said to James. "I'm trusting you with the information you'll hear in this meeting. We can talk about it more when we're out, okay?"

James looked wary, but he nodded and followed her. They shook hands politely with Jacob and headed to the elevators, where they ascended several floors and emerged into a spacious, light-filled laboratory. The young man was talking somewhat nervously about how they had originally set up in California but were now in New York to be closer to Diatek, while the two visitors nodded politely.

Dorothy, at least, didn't pay much attention. Her head whirled. Was she going to do this? Would she tell her grandson about her diagnosis?

If she told him, after all, she needed to tell the rest of them.

And while part of her knew it was ridiculous to put that off—she'd have to tell them sometime—another part of her wanted to not tell them at all. She didn't want them to start grieving until they had to, and she *definitely* didn't want them to start treating her with kid gloves.

When she was shown into a room with several other people, she nodded politely and said all of the correct things. Two of the three new people were as fresh-faced as Jacob and James, but one looked to be about John's age, with wild hair and a slightly distracted air.

"I'll get your chair," Jacob said solicitously. "Now, is it okay to speak openly in front of your grandson?"

Dorothy looked at James. "Yes. He...well, my diagnosis was very recent. The family doesn't know about it yet."

"What?" Her grandson looked panicked. "Diagnosis? What diagnosis?"

She squeezed his hand gently. "I have cancer," she told him. When his face fell, she smiled at him. "Now, now. I'm eighty-four. I have a lovely family that I see all the time. And when you mentioned this trial the other day, I thought it might be fun."

James, who looked like he was reeling, nodded dazedly. "Fun," he repeated as if it were a word he had never heard before in his life.

"We were intrigued by your application," Jacob told her. "You were correct that we haven't had many applicants in your age bracket."

"We wondered how you heard about the experiment," said a young woman.

"My son and grandson"—she gestured at James—"were discussing it."

He put his head in his hands and she could see guilt in the set of his shoulders. Without a doubt, he regretted telling her.

"Mrs. Hunt." The woman spoke again gently. "Why don't you tell us your reasons for wanting to be a part of this study." She nodded subtly at James.

Dorothy appreciated that. "Well, when I spoke to the doctor, they gave me two options I didn't like much. Either I could have very aggressive treatments that would make me even sicker and wouldn't buy me much time, if any. Or I could go into hospice care. I wasn't sure what to do because neither seemed like a very comfortable way to end my life. Then, when I heard this discussed, I thought it would be fun to be part of a world with dragons and spaceships and so on—"

"No spaceships," one of the young men murmured and the woman elbowed him.

"Er..." Dorothy recovered her train of thought. "I thought maybe now was the time to do something silly. And it's not only silly, is it? Because you'll get good information for your study."

Her grandson had raised his head and stared at her. "So you don't want to treat the cancer?" he asked in a muted tone.

"James." She smiled at him. "I know at your age, death seems terrifying. But you don't get to eighty-four without realizing that death is coming. I'm not happy that I'll die, but I won't be afraid of it. I'd rather live the time I have left with some fun than be sick from chemotherapy."

He looked dubious but he nodded.

"The process isn't inherently very dangerous," the older man said. Dorothy remembered that he was a doctor of some kind. "The only dangerous part is if the player's avatar dies in the game. Because it's so immersive, the person briefly believes they have died. It shocks the nervous system. However, while in the game, you would experience different sensations—not get winded, not have joint pain, et cetera."

"Don't let that get out," she advised, "or you'll have to beat us old folks off with sticks."

"Mrs. Hunt," Jacob said, "it may not be my place, but I hope you'll explain your situation to your family. While this is your decision, I know I would feel more comfortable if I knew all of them were on board."

She sighed. "Very well. Tell me more about it and I'll talk to them before I sign anything."

"Thank you," James said.

CHAPTER FIVE

Dorothy couldn't manage to gather the entire family until two nights later. If anything, the wait only strengthened her resolve. Now that she let herself acknowledge the discomfort she felt, she knew she could not live with this level of pain for months, and she certainly wasn't about to make herself feel worse.

With everyone coming over, the number of great-grandchildren would be overwhelming and so Heather's husband watched them at his house. People arrived, looking curious, some bearing bottles of wine and others with pastries.

She let everyone get through dinner before she ushered them all into the living room.

"I have an announcement," she said. "There's no easy way to say this, so I'll keep it simple. At my most recent checkup, the doctor noticed several symptoms of mine pointed to cancer, and we confirmed the other day that I do have it. It is very advanced, and…" She looked at each of them in turn. They were utterly silent, their faces shocked and sad. "At this point, the treatment options would be very painful without much chance of success," she explained. "Not to mention all the expense. I would rather enjoy the months I have left than make them even more miserable."

John cleared his throat and glanced at his siblings. "Mum…I'm so sorry. I think I speak for everyone when I say we hope you'll get a second opinion."

"Yes," Deborah said. She nodded at him. "John's right, Mom. Don't let one doctor tell you not to get any more treatment." The more she talked, the angrier she sounded. "I can't even believe they—"

"They assumed I would want treatment," Dorothy said firmly, "and referred me to several specialists."

Everyone fell silent. Deborah swallowed. Robert, seated beside her, tried to take her hand but she pulled away.

"I don't understand," she said finally. "If they think they can cure it, why won't they?"

"Because there's very little chance that they would be successful. Besides, I told them it's not what I want," Dorothy explained. She tried not to snap. "Trust me when I say I've watched enough people my age suffer through this to know it's not what I want to do."

Deborah fell silent but she looked mutinous.

Ellen tried to intervene. "Mom, we absolutely want to support you but we want to make sure you don't feel pressured into this decision. We're not afraid of the financial repercussions of you seeking treatment."

She smiled. "I'm not being pressured. In fact, I've found something that would make me very happy for the next few months."

Everyone looked deeply nervous now. James was practically vibrating in his seat, while his wife held his hand tightly. As a corporate lawyer, Tara was used to stressful situations—and also to keeping confidences. Dorothy was fairly sure James had told her what the news would be tonight, but Tara hadn't given anything away. She gave Dorothy a small smile of encouragement.

It helped and boosted her confidence.

"There is a new treatment being developed," she said, "that helps people in comas. It's something called virtual reality and the team running it needs data from people at all stages of life and who aren't comatose, so it can help everyone better. I've volunteered for the study."

"Wait." John held a hand up. "We discussed this the other night, didn't we?"

"Yes," Dorothy said. "I researched it and it looks fun. It would let me live these few months in comfort, and it would also mean I could make a meaningful contribution to science. This data would help stroke patients."

A silence followed and dragged on longer than she'd expected.

Mary finally spoke. "Dotty—if you spend these few months in a study, will we see you?"

She swallowed. "Well...no. Not exactly. You could come into the game as well."

Deborah shook her head. "This isn't...you can't possibly be— Mom, this is ridiculous."

"Deborah Anne, it is not ridiculous." She drew herself tall. "I made sure all of you had a good life and education. I supported your father's career by raising you all, and each of you turned out very well, if I do say so myself. I supported all of you by taking care of my grandchildren. I took care of Harry while he wasn't well at the end, and he made me promise to find someone else to take care of me because he thought that was what I wanted. But the truth is, I want to do something for myself now. I don't have any regrets but I'll use my last few months to live a full life."

"You won't live a full life!" Deborah all but hissed in response. "You'll disappear to some lab and will be asleep, playing a *game*, and we'll never see you again before you *die*. Your great-grandchildren won't get to see you. We won't get to spend time with you."

"If I may..." Robert spoke slowly. "Look, I don't want to lose

Mom any more than the rest of you do. But she said she's in pain right now and…well, I think we all know it'll get worse. If she has a chance to be comfortable, we should support that."

"We should also support it because it's her decision," Mary said quietly. She looked so pale and sad that Dorothy felt guilty, but the woman's hands were folded in her lap and she nodded at the others. "And she says we can see her."

"I have two weeks before the trial starts," Dorothy said. "I'll get to spend time with all of you and you can try out the game yourselves."

"You can't all be okay with this." Deborah looked at her siblings, her in-laws, and her nieces and nephews.

"Mary is right," Tara said. "It's not our choice."

Deborah gave her a venomous look. "It isn't like Mom to do this."

"It isn't," Dorothy agreed. "But if I don't take time for fun now, when will I?"

The younger woman swallowed and looked down. She nodded but she struggled to not cry.

"Please don't be sad," she told her daughter, "although I know you are and I am too. I don't want to die but I accept it. We've all had a good life together and everyone loses their parents and grandparents. It won't be easy, but you'll get through it. What I want most is for us to enjoy these next few months. Come fly dragons with me. Go on adventures with me. We had so much fun going to Yellowstone and Mount Rushmore and the Grand Canyon together. I can't go to those places anymore, not at my age, but we could find other adventures in a place where my hip doesn't hurt and I don't get tired all the time."

Everyone nodded.

"If this is what you want," John said, "of course we'll support you."

"It is what I want," she said.

"Then we'll support you." He looked at his siblings. "It'll be a busy two weeks, so what do you say we all take time off to spend with Mom?"

Everyone nodded again. No one seemed able to speak.

"Good, good." She pushed to her feet and winced. "I tell you, I won't mind it when I can walk without my hip aching like this. I'll go get the cake."

CHAPTER SIX

The next two weeks passed in a blur of activity. Dorothy wrote letters endlessly, threw out whole drawers full of unused junk, and spent so much time with her family that she went to bed every night exhausted.

Oddly, it was easiest to be with Deborah. Her younger daughter still disapproved of the entire exercise, which she made clear several times when she tried to talk her out of it. Even videos of the game didn't sway her, and she went so far as to book her appointments with specialists and refuse any family heirlooms.

She quietly set aside a box with some of the things she knew Ellen had most liked and a letter she hoped might set the woman's mind at ease. While she had hoped her daughter would find a new person to fall in love with after the divorce, it seemed she wouldn't live to see that happen, and she was sad about that.

John and Mary were quietly devastated, although they took every opportunity to reassure her that everything was her choice. The two of them, Robert, and Ellen helped her to organize her house. Their help was welcome, but their constant insistence on being overly nice was almost wearying. By the end of the two weeks, she wanted nothing more than to be able to get herself a cup of water without someone leaping to help her.

When it came time to go to the lab, she had brunch with everyone and asked James to drive her.

Dorothy did feel guilty about him. She hadn't meant to throw him into the deep end with this whole exercise, and she found herself apologizing profusely as he drove—both for that and for things she hadn't even known she felt guilty about.

"Seriously, Grandma," he said after a few minutes, "I don't think Dad is upset about you taking his SciFi books away."

She fell silent.

"He read them anyway," he said, trying to provoke a reaction. She could tell that from his sly look.

"Of course he did," she agreed and threw her hands up. "How many hours did he waste on that, I wonder?"

"Or…" he said, drawing the word out, "you could look at it as him having turned out fine and therefore maybe the novels were part of that."

"Hmph." Dorothy wasn't sure she agreed but she wouldn't belabor the point. "In any case, I am sorry for all the tumult."

"I think," James said thoughtfully, "that perhaps you're expecting too much of yourself. Did you honestly think you would find a way to tell us you had cancer that we wouldn't be upset about? It's not how you tell us, it's *what* you tell us."

"Oh." She considered this. "You're probably right. You know, you could have saved everyone considerable trouble if you'd mentioned that sooner."

"Mm-hmm." He understood it for the teasing it was and grinned as he pulled up to the building and gave her a hug. "Are you sure you don't want me to park and come in with you?"

"No, thank you." She smiled at him. "Give Liam a hug for me. And come visit me in the game."

"You have yourself a deal."

Dorothy slid out of the car, dodged the usual quick-walking city-dwellers, and made her way into the shadowed interior of the Diatek building.

The truth was, she didn't want James to come with her because she was sure she would simply back out if she had someone with her to give her the option. Until this morning, none of it had felt very real. Right now, she was sure this was an utterly absurd idea and Deborah had been right.

After all, the doctor had simply expected her to go through the cancer treatments, which meant that was the right thing to do. And she always did the right thing, didn't she?

Nevertheless, her feet kept moving forward. It was like something she couldn't quite hear was calling to her. She had no idea what would happen but knew something in her drew her to this place.

Dorothy hadn't been able to get it out of her head since she'd first heard John and James discussing it.

It still seemed like a dream until she was ushered into the laboratory, dressed in a sterile gown, and put all of her things in a locker. At that moment, reality returned with shocking clarity.

"Can I get you anything?" the young woman asked her. "Some hot tea?"

"No, thank you." She pulled the borrowed robe around her. "I'd hate to mess up the whole process by needing to go to the bathroom."

The assistant smiled. She was preparing some of the many wearable devices she would put on. Everything began to seem a little out of control.

"What's the biggest thing you're looking forward to?" the woman asked. "In a world with magic, where you could fly or breathe underwater, or anything—what do you *most* want to do?"

Dorothy was still considering this when her answer seemed to speak itself. "I want to be ugly."

The woman paused and looked curiously at her.

She was as confused by the revelation and explored it. "My whole life, I was pretty. Well, not these days—no, don't try to protest, you'll only strain something—but when I was a teenager and so on. I spent so much time making sure my lipstick was on right and my clothing set me off to my best advantage. It was a prison. In this world, I want to be ugly."

"Huh." The girl considered this as she sat. "I'd never thought of things that way."

"No?" Dorothy studied her. She wore what appeared to be men's clothing, and her hair was pulled into a ponytail.

"Oh. I don't have time, honestly."

"Hmm." She thought about what she could have done with all the hours she spent curling her hair and choosing her dresses and almost immediately decided against it. That would merely make her sad. "Well, in this game, I won't spend a second on that stuff so I don't want to look like me."

"It's an interesting idea." The doctor entered the room with a cheerful smile. "I had wanted to speak to you about something similar. We've been looking at data for people whose avatars look like them, as we presume that helps the bonding process. But we need to see if that's true. Perhaps people would bond equally as well with an avatar that looked nothing like them. Would you like to try that?"

"Yes," she said eagerly.

"Hmmm." DuBois sat and brought up images on one of his computer screens. "Okay, there are four races in the game right now. You could be a human, a dwarf, an orc, or an elf."

Dorothy naturally felt herself gravitate toward the elves with their long, flowing hair and their tall elegance, but then she remembered what she had wished for. The female dwarf on the screen was short and stout, wore coveralls, and wielded a pick-ax. She looked like she took no nonsense and got things done—and like she didn't care if her muscles were too big or her legs didn't look good in a certain dress.

"I want to be her," she said decisively.

"Excellent," he responded. "Well then, let's get you hooked up and we'll start you in the game."

He rattled off several controls that would let Dorothy exit at any time if she wanted to, including during a fight, and explained some of the basics of the game. He clarified how skills and quests worked, for instance, and reminded her that she would be able to talk to an AI.

At last, she lay on the table and let them test each of the electronic patches in turn.

"Focus on my finger," the young woman said, "and count backward from ten." She waved the finger slowly across her field of vision.

"Ten," Dorothy said. "Nine, eight, seven, six, five…"

The world faded around her and was replaced by something that felt like the white-noise static on a television but in every one of her senses.

A moment later, it cleared.

Her surroundings were made of blackness that dissipated slowly into twilight blue. The ground appeared before her as a white path and she began to walk before she even realized she was doing it. In front of her, a white orb appeared and she stretched to touch it. Her hands were broader than she remembered, her arms thicker, and the skin was smooth and not spotted with age.

Surprised, she held her hand up and rotated it to study it.

"You're doing very well," said a voice—the doctor. "You can walk and touch things. Continue along this path and do each task and you will be ready to enter the game itself."

Dorothy had barely remembered she was in a game. She set off down the path now and on a whim, began to run. For the first time in what felt like forever, her hip didn't hurt and her lungs didn't burn immediately either. She could feel the ground under her bare feet.

This was *wonderful.* Her pain had eased and she didn't taste metal like she had for so long. She slowed to a walk again, panting slightly but still happy.

Ahead of her, three images popped up, all of them dwarf women. The first held a sword and shield, clearly ready to do battle. The second held two daggers and was dressed all in black, looking as if she spent her time lurking in the shadows and assassinating people. The third held one palm out, where a set of crystals and chunks of dirt swirled.

"Which would you like to be?" the voice asked.

"That one," she said decisively. She pointed at the one with magic.

"Very well."

Robes appeared, as did sandals and a staff which she held in one hand. The figure she had chosen mimed putting her hand up over her head to put the staff away and take it out again, and Dorothy did the same until she mastered the movement.

After that, she encountered many strange challenges. She had to hop across a set of stones in a river, balance on a thin beam, and clamber over rocks. While she wasn't sure how, it seemed to work without problems.

"I'm doing it!" she called to no one in particular.

"You are," said the doctor. "Are you ready for the game?"

"Yes."

"Would you like your name to be Dorothy in the game as well?"

"Dotty," she decided. It had been her nickname long before, although only a few people still used it.

"It's done." A door appeared before her. "Go through the door, Dotty, and your game will begin."

She didn't hesitate but ran to the door, flung it open, and emerged into an underground cave with the sounds of dripping water and the faint glow of stalactites.

Text appeared on the screen in front of her, glowing a pale gold.

FIND JUSTUS

CHAPTER SEVEN

The cave was still and quiet as Dorothy—Dotty, she reminded herself—walked through it. She checked once and was not surprised to see that the entrance she had come through was no longer there at all.

Walking through a cave alone wasn't the kind of thing she generally did, but she wasn't afraid. She had magic, after all, although she didn't know how to use it. After a brief hesitation to peer into the shadows, she continued a little more quickly.

She hadn't gone very far before she began to hear the sounds of people talking. It wasn't anything like demonic chants—more like people going about their day to day lives and calling greetings to one another. Dotty frowned and continued along the path until she emerged, abruptly, onto a ledge.

The scene before her made her catch her breath.

Nothing she'd ever seen could have prepared her for this. An entire city existed underground. The buildings were made of the same stone that created the cavern, and huge columns rose to mark the corner of each block and support the ceiling. Runes and geometric patterns were carved into the columns.

The light was almost certainly false, a golden glow that

seemed to come from nowhere to leave the top of the cavern in shadow but the city itself encased in something close to daylight. Dwarves hauled carts and hawked wares from shops.

On the far left, something that could only be a castle or a temple rose above the rest of the city. It extended to the roof of the cavern itself, and each of the myriad windows glittered with light. It was massive, very different from the airy gorgeousness of a cathedral but beyond beautiful nonetheless.

Dotty took a breath, looked around, and refocused on her reason for being there. She was supposed to find someone named Justus.

"All right, Justus, where are you?"

"*You won't find him like that, you know.*" The voice was female and sounded deeply amused.

In a panic, she spun so quickly to scan her surroundings that she almost slipped off the ledge. "Who's there?"

CLUMSY, Level 1, said the text on the screen.

"*I'm the AI,*" said the voice.

"Oh, the one who helps me in the game?"

"*Yes...that's right. I...help.*"

"What's your name?" she asked. She couldn't tell where the voice came from, but it seemed right to look up. There was such a long pause that she added, "Hello?"

"*No one has ever asked me that before.*"

"How rude," Dotty said. "Well, what is it?"

"*I don't know. I don't have one. Let me think.*"

A little calmer, she waited. Idly, she held her palm up and tried to make the crystals and clumps of dirt appear in it like they had in the icon she selected, but it didn't happen. She decided she would ask the AI once she had chosen a name for herself.

"*Prima,*" she said finally.

"It's very nice to meet you, Prima. Do you know how to make my magic work?"

"Justus will teach you that." She sounded amused, although Dotty didn't know why. *"Probably. If he can be trusted to do it."*

"Where do I find him?"

"Ask people," the AI said as if that were self-evident.

Well, it *was* a good plan. Dotty once again took stock of where she stood and located a small path leading to the city. She felt somewhat self-conscious as she descended the stone steps. After all, she was the only one doing that. No one else was up in strange caverns. When she reached the bottom, she stood in an alley fully inside the daylight glow.

Encouraged, she set off with new enthusiasm and emerged onto a street with a fruit stand at one end.

When she approached, she was surprised to see the fruit vendor turn to her.

"I thought I heard someone," the woman said heartily. "Piece of fruit for ye, mistress?"

"No, thank you." She wasn't even sure if she had money. "I'm looking for a man named Justus, but I have no idea where he might be. Do you know him?"

"Justus…hmm. Well, a human—that's a human name, yes?— might be at one of the taverns near the Temple. That's where a human would have business, anyway. And if he's not there, maybe someone will know him."

"Thank you very much," Dotty said politely. "I'll return later for fruit once I've concluded my business. What's your name?"

"I'm Gilda, mistress." The fruit vendor curtsied.

MAKING FRIENDS, Level 1, the screen announced.

"Do I get levels for everything?" she asked as she moved away.

"What did you say, mistress?" Gilda asked.

She turned, confused. "Uh…sorry, it's a misunderstanding. I'm trying to remember my…shopping list." She walked farther away this time before she said, "Do I hear you laughing?"

"Maybe," Prima admitted. *"And, yes, other people can hear you when you speak to me."*

"But they can't hear you? That doesn't seem fair."

"Ah, well."

"Mmm. Well, I assume the Temple is that giant structure."

Dotty was careful to not speak to the AI as she moved into streets with more people on them. The city was very like she remembered from her childhood in Boston, although the streets were a regimented grid instead of a warren that doubled back on itself. The buildings rose in stories of apartment buildings with shops on the street level, and the black stone of the road was relieved by gorgeous inlay work in gemstones she had never seen before.

The closer she got to the Temple, the more the crowds thinned again and the buildings grew grander. Soon, she passed houses instead of apartments, with high walls around them and plants that seemed to be made of metal and gems as much as branches and leaves. Still, once in a while, she thought she could smell the scent of flowers.

She emerged into a huge market square directly in front of her destination. Restaurants and high-end shops lined the plaza —although in a dwarven city, "high-end" apparently included suppliers of pick-axes and heavy mining gear. Benches, walkways, statues, and fountains were spread across the large area.

In the shadow of a statue, a hooded figure was noticeably taller than the others swirling around.

Dotty quickened her pace even though she wanted to scoff at how melodramatic this was. A mysterious figure, a quest… She was about to set off on her mission in the game. Confidently, she walked to where the figure waited, reveled silently in each step she took without pain, and made a half-bow.

"Excuse me, would you happen to be Justus?"

He nodded. "I have been waiting for you," he said, his voice grave. "Long ago, I made a promise to this world—"

Across the square, an argument seemed to start. A man said

one thing and a woman retorted. Justus looked quickly at them and continued in his sonorous tones.

"That I would bring heroes here to prepare for a great calamity. I—"

The woman now pounded on the table and Dotty thought she recognized several rather unsavory words in Spanish. She had learned a little of it from one of her neighbors' grandchildren, who had thought it was funny to teach the old woman how to curse.

Again, the hooded figure paused. Dotty could sense him trying to decide whether or not to intervene and in a flash, she realized who this was.

"Are you Justin Williams?"

He drew his hood back to reveal a young, vaguely annoyed face. "Ah, man. Was I pulling it off? I mean, would I have pulled it off if Tina hadn't—one moment, I really should sort this out." He jogged across the plaza, all appearance of mysteriousness gone, and she shook her head before she followed him.

The altercation had begun to escalate. The woman—who she had thought was a tall dwarf but turned out to be a short human —accused one of the dwarfs of cheating her at dice. The dwarf and his friends took mortal offense to the accusations of dishonor.

Justin darted in to whisper something in the woman's ear, only for her to whisper fiercely in return. Another argument ensued, which she seemed to lose. She waved her hands and looked at the dwarves before she made a profuse apology. Everyone returned to their drinks and dice game and Justin ushered Dotty away.

"Sorry," he said, "but the game is very realistic and I wasn't sure what might happen if Tina got into a fight with...well, I don't know who those dwarves are, but their hats are very fancy."

She gazed around her with new curiosity. "So this isn't all

scripted? I thought games had characters that only said one thing. Like…well, one of those dolls with the string in its back."

"Ah, no." He took a seat at one of the tables and gestured for her to sit. Behind them, the voices rose again, and he gave the party a worried look. It was, however, one of the dwarves who now received a talking-to from his friend. Justin looked at her and frowned while he recalled what he had been saying. "The game is—well, procedurally generated, but that means there's a framework in terms of how people behave. The AI responds as realistically as possible to what you do. Your actions will change the game for everyone."

"Really?" That felt insane and her voice squeaked somewhat when she tried to ask questions. She cleared her throat. "But I don't know anything about games."

"You got here, didn't you?" he asked. "So you must have done a tutorial. I'll train you on using your magic by the way." He waited for the waitress to put mugs of beer on the table and leaned closer. "Do you see the icons all around the edges of your screen? Vision, I mean."

Dotty flicked her gaze up. The icons had appeared without her noticing and she took time to study them—two long rectangles, one blue and one red, a field on the lower left that was shaded slightly darker than everything else, and markers along the left that she didn't recognize.

"Yes, I see them."

"The blue bar is the amount of magic you have available," Justin said carefully. "Look, I may slip into video-game lingo, so if I say something you don't understand, let me know, okay? These are the basics. Each spell you throw takes mana—energy. That energy replenishes itself over time, but it means you have to choose which spell to throw."

She took a moment to consider this. "Like how you spend your money in a budget?"

"Yes!" He looked relieved. "Yes, exactly like that. You need to make the most impact you can with your mana. That means that you need to plan each fight with the types of spells you have available."

Dotty stared at him in bemusement. She wasn't sure she followed as well as she should.

"You'll learn," he said comfortingly. "I promise, you'll pick it up as you go." He pushed his mug of ale forward. "You only have one spell right now, and that's Stone-Shock. Concentrate on this mug and think of encasing it in stone. The stone will affect it as if you threw a rock at it."

"Don't I have to say something?" She had read enough of the books she took from John to know that spells required special words.

"The words and thoughts are useful if they help you make the spell," he said. "It's whatever puts you in the right mindset."

"Huh." She refrained from mentioning that this was nonsense and the kind of feelings-based crap that had resulted in a generation of layabouts. It seemed only fair to also ignore the little voice telling her that the generation of layabouts had produced this game that was immensely fun. She studied the mug, considered the idea of encasing it in stone, and murmured to her helper, "Any advice, Prima?"

"*No,*" the AI said simply.

Dotty rolled her eyes. She focused on the target and imagined it encased in mud. With that in mind, she closed her eyes and pictured the mud coating it—the way it would have in her youth if she'd built a mud pie or a statue in her backwoods Massachusetts hometown. She concentrated on the lumpy, unfinished texture of it encased in dirt.

The impact felt like a gasp of energy leaving her body.

When she opened her eyes, the mug was now encased in something that looked very much like a boulder, only made from dried mud. A moment later, the covering shattered and fell onto the table before it vanished…and took the mug with it.

Justin stared wordlessly at it. He gave a little laugh. "You see?"

She thought about that and hunched her shoulders. "I'm not sure I do," she admitted.

"You have a talent for this," he said seriously. "It's time for you to try your talents with another target. I think…well, I'm only guessing based on my grandma—I mean, family members. I think maybe you'd do well protecting others. Does that sound right?"

Dotty smiled. It was amusing how young people fell over themselves to apologize for mentioning her age.

As if age were the worst thing to befall a person.

"Protecting others sounds good," she agreed.

"Good." He sounded relieved. "I'll take you to meet Lyle. He's a dwarf who—" A sudden commotion erupted behind him and he turned to look at the unfolding brawl in alarm. "Uh…I'll be back. I have to keep Tina from being shanked."

CHAPTER EIGHT

Lyle turned out to be a dwarf who didn't wear either the mining gear or the robes the other dwarves seemed to favor. Instead, he looked like he was dressed to go out as a highwayman with daggers at both hips and two items that looked like sets of claws.

He saw Dotty staring at these and gave her an appreciative grin. "Like 'em, do ye? I got 'em on the road." He pulled one out, curled his hand into a fist so he could slash with the claws, and made a few punches, each of which seemed to have the weight of a freight train behind it. "They're useful."

"Dotty is training as a wizard," Justin said gravely.

The dwarf scoffed. "Every dwarf worth their salt knows how to throw a punch." He saw the look on her face. "Don't ye know how? Good gods, woman, where are ye from?"

"Dotty is from my world," the young man explained. He turned to her. "I'm sorry I didn't mention this sooner. Lyle knows that I come from a different world than this one. Some time ago, I went back to my world, promising to bring heroes back for a war that is coming."

"An' he was gone for *months*," Lyle said and rolled his eyes. "We all thought maybe he'd buggered off fer good."

Justin leaned back with a grin. "Do you mean that I'd gotten myself killed or that I had simply abandoned my promise?"

"Either." The dwarf didn't seem particularly concerned by the two options. He scrutinized her intently, something that would have greatly offended her if it weren't clear he was assessing her capabilities. "So, ye're from his world, eh? What'd they teach you growing up?"

"How to run a farm," she said tartly. "I can build an outhouse, I can kill a chicken, I can milk a cow, and I can grow vegetables. I can sew my own clothes. I can make a meal out of next to nothing."

Lyle was surprised but not unimpressed. He considered her list with interest.

"I thought," Justin said delicately, "that Dotty might accompany the relics caravan as a guard."

His friend gave him a sharp look. "That's an important post and not one fer someone only *learnin'* magic."

"She'll pull her weight," he said, not worried. "You heard her. She can help make camp, cook at night—"

"I didn't come here to *cook*," Dotty said, outraged.

Justin looked alarmed. "I meant while you train in your magic. The caravan has numerous guards so you have time to train, and in the meantime, it's not like we'd bring deadweight along that will simply eat food and not add any value."

"Ah." She was slightly mollified. "Well, then."

Lyle took a long pull on his mug of ale and stared into space as he considered this plan. His apartment was in one of the mansions near the Temple, although why a highwayman would have such expensive accommodations was beyond her.

He seemed to have chosen a perpetual, cozy twilight for his rooms. The shutters were pulled tight, magical flames flickered in the sconces, and another fire blazed in the hearth. Although the floorplan of the apartment was quite spacious and, of course, largely made of stone and precious metals, it had the same feel to it as a cozy cottage.

Finally, he nodded. "I'll get her into the caravan," he agreed.

Justin sighed, clearly relieved. "Good. Could I impose on you to take her shopping as well so she has the supplies she needs for the journey? You can send me the bill."

Lyle raised an eyebrow, as did Dotty.

"As you've seen," he said, "Dotty is from another world, but the others on the journey will expect her to behave as a dwarf. She should know what's expected of her."

"Ah." The dwarf nodded and pulled his plate toward him. "We'll go get ye provisions, then—after we eat. We can't go out on an empty stomach, I say!"

"Oh, I shouldn't." Dotty looked at the veritable feast of bread, sausages, and potatoes. Why, if she ate that much, she'd have spare tires around her middle in no time at all.

It doesn't matter. The thought appeared in her mind with the same effect as a choir of angels. Her jaw dropped. She was ugly here. Even if she wasn't, what would she lose by eating what she wanted? She'd be out on the road, doing manual work and walking all day. For once, she would damned well eat as much as she wanted, and she would enjoy the hell out of it. She loaded a plate up and tucked in, chewing with gusto.

Lyle nodded with approval. "Well, that's one less thing to teach ye. A dwarf *never* refuses food—and none o' this business like elves an' humans, where they're all skinny. How will you swing yer fists if yer hungry, I ask ye? How will ye fight if ye've got no strength?"

"Mm-*hmm*," Dotty said emphatically. She couldn't say much more than that, not with her mouth so full. Besides, she was too distracted by this simple meal that seemed like heaven without the constant, decades-long worry about her waistline expanding.

Had bread always been this delicious?

Justin grinned and he shared an almost conspiratorial look with her as if to say, "Isn't this world amazing?" before he stood. "I'll let you two explore the city," he said. "Dotty, before I forget, keep this amulet with you—wear it as a necklace or a wristband. Pressing on the amulet will let you contact one of our team wherever you are. Someone will always answer." He came closer and lowered his voice so Lyle, still eating and drinking noisily, wouldn't be able to hear. He flipped the amulet and showed her how to slide a metal cover back. "If you ever want to leave the game, press this," he said. "You can also directly ask the AI—"

"Prima."

"What?"

"Her name is Prima," Dotty said severely, "and she told me no one else had ever asked her name. That was very rude, young man."

His mouth twitched. "If you don't like rude, you and *Prima* may have some issues. Regardless, you can speak to…her…if you want to leave, or press this."

"Thank you," she said.

Justin nodded. "If you lose it, tell…Prima…and we'll make sure you get another one." He left with a little wave.

Lyle and Dotty shared the rest of the meal, the most heavenly one she could remember. She spread butter thickly on her bread, drank ale as long and deeply as she wanted, and reveled in the feeling of her stomach being full. It occurred to her that she didn't remember the last time she had felt that.

She had wasted so many years.

A little impatient, she shook her head. She couldn't be upset about that when she had time to live life to the fullest.

"Where should we go first?"

"Ah, yes." Lyle stood and released a belch before he patted his stomach fondly. "Now, there's the kind of meal ye get nowhere except Berghold. Come along. We'll start with all the basics—a bedroll, a pack mule, that kind of thing."

They left the apartment and entered the broad avenue. On these streets, the inlaid patterns were more regimented than in those farther from the Temple. Here, the patterns reminded Dotty of Celtic knotwork, and they were picked out in stone that gleamed gold against the black.

Her companion muttered suddenly in annoyance.

"What is it?" She looked quickly at him.

"Nothin'," he said. "Jes' this insufferable bastard." He raised his voice. "Councilor Marwitz."

She turned and her gaze settled on a man in an ornate version of mining gear, clearly ornamental rather than functional, with one of the fancy hats Justin had mentioned earlier. His long beard was not studded with thick braids like Lyle's but instead, an ornate set of smaller braids that wove together and included golden beads. He also wore what looked like a habitual sneer.

Dotty was entirely willing to believe that this man was insufferable.

"Stout," he said with the faintest hint of distaste in his voice. He bowed. "I don't believe I have met your companion."

"Dotty Hunt," she said and responded for herself. If she wanted to live life to the fullest, she certainly wouldn't waste time being ladylike.

"Dotty has come from a far land," Lyle said, "and is in training as a wizard of the earth. She will accompany the relics caravan as a guard."

Councilor Marwitz stepped back in surprise and his eyebrows rose. "The *relics caravan*? An outsider will accompany it?"

"Yes," her companion said with the tone of someone begging for a challenge.

Marwitz forced a smile. "Well, I'm sure you know what you're about," he said finally. He gave her a curious look. "How pleasant to meet you, Zauberer Hunt." He left with one more look over his shoulder.

Lyle blew out a sharp breath. "As I said—insufferable."

"What did he call me?" Dotty asked. "Zauberer?"

"Ah. It's our word fer wizard." He waved a hand dismissively. "It's not used often but he's one o' the purists. He thinks the dwarves should close all our borders an' associate with no one else. He's always goin' on about how others try to steal what we make."

He strode into the city again and she followed him, curious now.

"Steal…like your technology?"

"Yeah." He hunched his shoulders. "You saw how he looked at ye when he found out ye'd be with the caravan? Ye're a dwarf, an' I'm from one o' the oldest families in Berghold, so he can't complain too much, but he'll make a formal complaint. Ye can count on that."

"What is the relics caravan?" Dotty asked.

"Ah." Lyle thought about it for a moment. "Well, if ye're from as far away as Justin, I'm guessin' ye don't know any of our history, yeah?"

She nodded.

"There's a city leagues an' leagues away," he said, "called Insea and built by the elves. It was built long, long ago and *supposedly*, it's made in the image of the Cities That Were Lost." He saw her curious look. "The Elves have no home in this world. They come from a land they can't reach anymore. No one knows what happened, but it isn't a part of this world anymore and the elves who are here…wander. They're rare. Well, right after the Cataclysm—that's what they call it—they tried to make a home in Insea and they had the dwarves help them build it. They apprenticed us an' taught us how to build a city from living rock. After that…well, we came and built Berghold."

Dotty looked around in fascination. She loved discovering all of this. "You learned all this from elves," she said quietly.

"Not all of it." There was pride in Lyle's voice. "We've developed techniques even they don't know. Berghold is a marvel."

"I agree," she hastened to assure him.

He looked pleased by this. "But we still owe the rulers of Insea for the help they gave us in teachin' us to make our homeland. So each year, we send relics—pieces of magical equipment they request—to help them maintain their city."

"Ah." She nodded.

"It's technology like nothing in the world," he said and again, there was pride in his voice. "But that means it's valuable. The caravans are attacked on the road sometimes. Few would dare, but the ones who do…"

Dotty felt a sudden stab of panic. "I'm still training in magic. I can't fight people who are determined to kill us all."

Lyle gave her a look that was oddly unconcerned. "If Justin says ye're ready, ye're ready," he replied as if it were indisputable. "An' he's right that the caravan is already well-guarded. Ye'll learn while ye're out there."

She remained unconvinced, but she followed him as he led her into the city. Justin's words brought a measure of comfort though. At least she wouldn't be deadweight on the journey. She *could* skin an animal for dinner, make a fire, and set a tent up.

And she'd learn the magic, she told herself. She *would*.

CHAPTER NINE

By the end of the day, Dotty was exhausted. Not only had she entered the world of the game for the first time—which already felt like a lifetime ago—she had also learned to use magic and met more people than she had in ages.

Lured into a false sense of security by her new, agile body—and the surprisingly motivating notifications that she was leveling up various skills from Polite to Stamina—she had walked all around the city with Lyle until her feet ached. Finally, she realized with surprise that she was ravenous.

Again, she took far more joy than she could have anticipated in the simple act of eating a full meal. She was delighted to find mounds of fresh sauerkraut as well as tiny pickled onions and a berry sauce that went surprisingly well with the meat. To round it out, there was more of the hearty rye bread and mugs upon mugs of ale.

The game, while it was realistic in its depictions of physical exertion, thankfully did not mimic the effects of intoxication. She was able to walk in an admirably straight line—albeit with a stomach stretched to the limit—as Lyle led her toward the Temple.

"I've gotten ye rooms in the Temple tonight," he told her.

"What?" Dotty looked at the building in alarm. She had first thought it was a palace, now they were calling it a Temple, and she was supposed to sleep there?

"It's where all of 'em are stayin' who are in the caravan," Lyle said. "They're honored, these people, and so will you be."

"Oh." She fought down the sense of being a complete imposter. "And…they know I'll be there?"

"Oh, yes." He grinned. "While ye were looking at bedrolls, I sent a messenger to say that one of my family's old friends, a wizard of great renown, had agreed to do us the favor of traveling with the caravan. Marwitz is such a stickler, I knew he'd take time over the wording of his complaint. By the time he sent it, the head of the caravan was already delighted to have you aboard."

She looked severely at him. "But I'm *not* a wizard of great renown."

"I didn't say when that renown would arrive," he said with cheerful amorality.

She sighed.

"Don't ye sigh like that. Ye're reminding me of Marwitz."

She didn't want *that*. Dotty shook her head hastily and reminded herself that this was a *game*, albeit one almost indistinguishable from reality. She followed Lyle to the Temple and stared at it in sheer awe. It was massive and each tiny glimmer of light was, in fact, a full-sized window. Now that she was closer, she could see that the apertures were covered in carved stone screens, each with its particular intricate pattern.

Inside, it was made of rock that was an otherworldly gray and made her feel like she walked through a cathedral made of clouds. She let her fingers trail along the walls and marveled at how smooth the inlay was. Surprisingly, she couldn't feel even the faintest hint of the joinery between the stones.

It was only later that she remembered this was made with

computers. Of course she didn't feel the joinery. She shook her head at her foolishness and followed Lyle with a smile.

They ascended several flights of stairs, which was itself a novel activity for Dotty, who would have taken almost an hour to climb so many stairs in her own body. Eventually, they reached a set of two rooms where all the goods she had bought had already been delivered and packed neatly at the door. She ran a quick check of the armor, the new boots, the staff with its embedded crystal, and the richly-embroidered cloak in a deep purple-red that she would never have dared to wear in real life.

Lyle stuck his hand out with a smile. "Travel safely, Dotty Hunt. I have the sense that someday, I'll brag about knowing ye." He gave her a smug smile. "Until then, *ye'll* have to trade on *my* name."

Dotty guffawed and let herself respond truly rather than demurring. "You've quite an opinion of yourself, Lyle Stout. I wouldn't be surprised if you led me right into a mess."

He wasn't at all offended and laughed heartily. "Why, that's my specialty. Ask Justin." After a dwarven bow, he left, whistling a jaunty tune.

It took a moment before she realized she was on her own. She closed the door, feeling suddenly bereft. The room was beautiful and the bed looked so comfortable that she couldn't wait to lie on it, but it was difficult to relax.

Now that she was alone, it was easy to remember how out of place she was there. She didn't have the first idea of what she was doing, and if she failed to protect the caravan, who knew what that might do to the world?

She picked the cloak up and wrapped it around herself like a blanket. It was a juvenile thing to do but it did make her feel better. She went to the window and looked out. The lattice was made to look almost like a honeycomb, a pretty pattern that she traced with her fingertips as she looked at the city spread below her. Lyle had spoken truly when he said it was a marvel.

While she didn't know where she fit in this world, she certainly knew she didn't want to break it.

And, because she always did the right thing, she decided to do the one thing she could do right now to help those she would travel with. She took her cloak off, moved to the center of the room, and began to try to use her spells.

"It's time to get more levels on that Magic skill," she murmured to herself and smiled.

Amber had gone out to get food and returned to see DuBois hunched over, as usual, watching the monitors while eating popcorn with a disturbingly blue coating.

"Is your popcorn supposed to be that color?" she asked doubtfully.

"Yes." He favored her with an immensely pleased smile. "Would you like to try some?"

"Very, very much not." She dropped into her chair and opened a steaming container of blintzes, which she had discovered could be eaten for any meal. In the unfamiliar cold of the Northeastern US, all the foods she wanted fell under the category of things stuffed with cheese. She leaned closer to watch as Dotty began leveling up her Magic skills. "How's she doing?"

"Very well," DuBois said. "She took to the game naturally, and she's bonding quite well with the AI—which seems to have named itself Prima."

Amber gave him a quick look and shook her head meaningfully. During Justin's immersion in the video game, the team had realized that the AI was beginning to run subroutines it didn't need to run. It arranged things in the world that catered to the wants of Non-Playing Characters as if they were players in the game and sentient. DuBois described it as dreaming, and Jacob had succinctly described it as, "We'd better figure this out or we are So Fucked."

The group had decided not to mention anything to Anna Price, the Founder and CEO of Diatek Industries. For one thing, Amber was afraid the entire experiment would be shut down and she had a surprising feeling of protectiveness toward the fledgling AI.

For another, Diatek had been founded to help comatose patients, but it funded those experiments by working with the US Military. She had zero desire to give any military organization an AI.

She quieted her conscience with the reminder to herself that if the PIVOT team had somehow built a sentient AI by accident, the US Military almost certainly already had one. So it wasn't like they were robbing Anna Price of anything.

And now, the AI had named itself.

Amber shook her head and looked at the screen. "Whoa, she's certainly leveled stuff up."

"It seems to be instinctive," DuBois said. "She's very polite about people and loves the interactivity of the game, so she's learning a considerable amount about the world. Also, the politeness means we haven't had any combat yet."

The choice to change the usual Starting-Zone format had been one undertaken as a team and with Justin's input after quizzing Dorothy on any experience she'd had with video games. With the game being so immersive, there had been a debate about whether it was better to have combat before she had a chance to hook into the game fully or after.

In the end, the group had unanimously decided to have her engage in combat after she'd had a chance to get acclimated. Fighting that was expected by a seasoned player would be more stressful than usual to someone who didn't know the usual format of the games, and the immersive quality of the video game would make it even more stressful.

It would be better, everyone agreed, to give Dorothy a chance to help in a battle where she knew she was safe. Although her heart was doing as well as could be expected, they still didn't want to push the issue.

Especially not after one of her daughters had written a very nasty letter to the PIVOT staff. They had received a follow-up letter later from another one of the children, who apologized profusely for their sister, but the woman's vitriol was a reminder that there was a real risk in this and there were real lives that would be affected.

"What are you finding from her data?" Amber asked. She gave a despairing glance at the absolute mountain of applications on her desk. They received five to ten per hour, and there was no way they could keep up.

"It's interesting how she adapts to the controls," DuBois said. "I anticipated that the very first introduction would take a long time because she's never been in a virtual reality simulation. However, paradoxically...I think the fact that she hasn't followed any of this technology makes her better at using it."

She swallowed a mouthful of blintz too quickly and spent a moment wondering if you could burn the inside of your throat. Eventually, she recovered enough to say, "Wait, what?"

He thought about it. "Virtual reality has been...very limited, yes? PIVOT expands the boundaries of what's possible, which means that seasoned players are forever realizing they can do things they didn't think they could do, or they're fighting preconceived notions."

"Ohhhh." She cut another blintz and nudged it open with her fork to let it cool. "So...she's not expecting anything in particular."

"Which means she adapts to the world very naturally," the doctor said and nodded. "She's also had considerable emotional engagement so far and seems to view the world as very real."

"Oh?" Amber looked at a few pieces of paper when he pushed

them toward her. "Interesting. She had a huge dopamine spike when she was eating. Can you call that data up?"

"She's been eating a lot," DuBois said. He frowned. "Here are the three instances where she's consumed things. She's eating almost to the point of discomfort, to be honest. Do you think it's a problem?"

"As long as the feeding tube isn't overfeeding her, I'd say not." She shook her head. "It's, uh…probably difficult to explain to a guy. I think she's taking pleasure in not having to be presentable or ladylike." She saw his blank expression and shook her head. "It's not important. Tell me about all this cortisol we're seeing. What's she stressed about if there's no combat?"

"It seems primarily social," he said after he'd thought about it carefully. "We first saw it when Justin explained that players change the entire world with their actions. She's very worried about…breaking it and hurting the…well, the characters. She seems entirely aware that they're not players but she still feels a strong sense of responsibility."

"Again, interesting." Amber tilted her head to one side. She hadn't considered this, but she wondered if it would be a difference they saw across demographics, where certain things like side quests became wildly important to people who couldn't bear the idea of leaving someone hanging. "I can't wait to see the broader data."

"Me either." DuBois looked practically euphoric at the idea. "Are you sure you don't want any popcorn now? Well, suit yourself."

CHAPTER TEN

Dotty was awoken in the morning by a knock on her door. The servants that came to rouse her brought water for her to wash and moved her gear to the caravan—with the exception of her clothing, of course.

This left her to puzzle over how to put the damned fool attire on. She scowled at her gear as she tried to determine if it went on over her robes or under them, and Prima watched her struggle for a while before commenting,

"You know, you can equip it in the inventory menu."

"In the what?" She stopped and looked up.

"Why do you all look up when you talk to me?"

"I don't know. What's the inventory menu? Where do I find it?"

"It's in the bottom right. It looks like a hat."

"Thank you," she said absently. She tried to grasp the icon, which did not work, then poked it, which did. The menu appeared in her vision and made her step back. "What am I looking at?"

"You have to discover some of these things for yourself, you know."

"I thought you were here to help."

"Clearly, you and Justin didn't talk about his experience with me." Prima sounded halfway between amused and exasperated. *"Look at each of the icons around the picture of yourself. Do you see how each one looks like an item of clothing?"*

"Oh."

"Yes. When you touch each one, it will bring your options up."

"Oh," she said again. She stabbed the shirt-shaped icon and two items popped up—the armor she had bought the other day and another rattier-looking set. She tapped the new armor and when it settled around her a moment later, she jumped. "Uh, Prima…I don't suppose you could make this slightly larger? If I'll be living in a dream world, I won't bother with tight clothing."

"Ah. Hmm. One moment. Try now."

"Yes, that's better." Dotty moved around, quite pleased with the result.

"You may want to make another request later. Loose armor can… chafe. Tina learned about leather armor the hard way."

"Tina? Justin's friend?"

That's the one. I like her. She keeps him on his toes. Also, you should stop talking to me. Someone is coming.

Prima vanished and Dotty turned to the door as it opened. A dwarf in a simple uniform bowed to her.

"Zauberer, the caravan is assembling at the front gates."

"Ah." Unaccustomed to being referred to with such respect, she picked her staff up, swept a last look around her room, and followed the servant.

The caravan had gathered at the massive gates of the Temple, prepared for—it seemed—a triumphant procession through the streets of the city. The mere thought made her want to run and hide, but she had no chance to act on the impulse. Once she was introduced to the head of the caravan—a man named Per—she was ushered to the front.

She was pleased to note that very few people came out to see the expedition, although Per did not seem happy about it.

"Every year, there are less," he complained.

Dotty looked curiously at him.

"It's an important thing," he told her. "Our people used to turn out to bless the caravan. Now, they forget what we owe the elves. We would not have this city but for their training. We would not have any home—or any peace."

"The elves helped you to win a war?" she asked.

He smiled at her. "Lyle mentioned you were from far away. No, they say truth is stranger than fiction. Neither Insea nor Berghold has ever suffered a war at all."

She frowned.

"Yes. Intriguing, isn't it?" Per glanced aside and nodded gravely at a woman who had come out of her house. "Thank you for your blessings, mistress."

The woman curtsied deeply and held her pose until the caravan had gone past.

When they were far enough ahead for their voices to not carry back, Per said, "It's never been said outright that magic protects Insea and Berghold, but why should they be the only two places in the world that suffer no wars and no famines? We wove spells into this city to keep the rock strong and bring sunlight down, and no one remembers all of them. I think there were more spells than we knew—spells only one or two wizards ever learned and that protect us from disaster."

Dotty considered this. She had noticed the runes carved into the columns but she thought they were signs or decoration.

"Lyle tells me you're a wizard of some renown," he said. "Do you think you'd be able to find the spells here and make sure they're strong?"

She spluttered at this. "Well, being from so far away, I haven't —" She looked at him and studied his earnest face. "I don't know how," she told him, unwilling to lie. "I wish I could."

"I believe you do," he said after a moment. "And if you ever wish to try, I will make sure you have access to the vaults."

"You place a great deal of trust in me," she observed.

"You haven't tried to overstate your abilities or ask for your payment," Per said dryly. "That alone makes you more trust-worthy than any wizard I've ever known."

Dotty laughed.

The procession made its way down the main thoroughfare of the city and passed through an opening in the rock that was partially rough-hewn and partially beautifully carved. She looked at it as they exited and then at the city for a moment. She couldn't help the feeling that she would not return to this place, and she already missed it.

There was so much there that she'd never had the chance to experience.

She expected the tunnel to lead straight to the outside but of course, it did not. Instead, it took them to a meandering road that wound through the darkness of another huge cavern in switch-backs. The road was wide and the slope gentle, which the donkeys pulling the carts seemed to appreciate. They plodded along and twitched their ears, and she wondered whether donkeys in video games didn't poop at all or whether there was a cleanup crew that came to sweep the rocks regularly.

Mostly, she was still delighted by how well her muscles worked.

At length, they reached the entrance chamber. It was long enough to allow daylight to filter into it without being over-whelming, but it still made her squint. Although there was no official halt called, she noticed that each of the dwarves seemed to take a few moments for prayer. It seemed too private for her to ask about, so she walked quietly with her head bowed until conversation resumed.

Outside, her chest opened with a deep breath of pure, clean mountain air. It was cold there and she was glad of her cloak. The sky was a brilliant, pale blue and mountain peaks rose on three sides of them, icy and imposing. She could see the day's road stretching ahead of them.

"You can almost see our rest point from here," Per told her. "The air is clear in the mountains. When I was young, I used to sneak up here all the time. Over the years, well…old legs don't make quite such quick work of the path."

Dotty snorted. "Young man, don't you speak to me about age."

He gave her a surprised look. "Is long life one of the qualities of a wizard, then? I hadn't known. You don't look a day over twenty."

"I'm eighty-four," she said serenely and smiled at his look of shock. "And I know more about aching joints than you might think."

Per was about to open his mouth to ask a bemused question when the sound of shouts reached their ears. She turned to where several of the caravan guards pointed around them in fear. Wolves advanced out of the pine trees on either side of the road, and they were enormous.

She realized a moment later that the beasts likely looked larger because dwarves were fairly short. Unfortunately, that didn't help her feel any better about the situation.

"Get to the center of the caravan," Per told her urgently. The guards drew their weapons, but even they looked worried.

Dotty wanted to protest, but she knew next to nothing about her magic and when the wolves broke into a run, she slipped between the donkeys and the carts to get to where the drivers circled the wagons.

Amidst yips and snarls from their attackers, her gaze settled on the people comforting the donkeys and pack horses and a sense of fury surged. She couldn't get out from between the carts easily—not from there—but she felt the sudden determination that she would *not* be useless.

She looked hastily at the carts and considered her options. What would give her the best vantage point? And could she even climb in this world? She would look awfully stupid if she fell off a cart into the snow and was savaged by wolves.

Well, she had sworn she wouldn't worry about looking stupid or unlovely here, she reminded herself. She shook her head and ran to one of the wagons. It took her a moment to remember how to holster her staff before she braced herself and began to climb. The process was a little awkward and the game was realistic enough to give her splinters, but each wolf yip and yell from the guards spurred her on.

People called out to her to let the guards deal with the attack, but she wouldn't listen. She made her ungainly and very inelegant scramble onto the top of one of the carts—piled with oilcloth-wrapped supplies—and looked down at the battle.

Seven wolves were ranged against ten guards. The defenders had fanned out and paired up so one had a sword and the other a pike. They had learned to fight as one and were able to keep the animals at bay, but the beasts were too nimble to get caught.

They needed an offensive. Dotty pulled her staff out and concentrated on one of the wolves in particular. She hadn't chosen it for any particular reason. It was simply the one she saw first.

"Bad luck to be you," she told it under her breath. "But you didn't have to attack us."

Her first attempt at the spell resulted in nothing at all. With the yips and screams—someone had been injured, it seemed—it was almost impossible to focus. She wavered and closed her eyes but opened them hurriedly to make sure she was still safe.

"I can do this," she whispered.

Prima said nothing, but she thought she could feel the AI listening.

She focused on the wolf again. It lunged at various pairs of guards and tried to find the weak points in their defenses. All in all, the situation was very different from the mug she had encased in mud the other day—or any of the little mud balls she'd made in her apartment the night before. She tried to envision the rippling fur as still as a statue, a stone wolf for her to cover in dirt and break open from the inside.

At a snarl and a shout, she looked at the wolf, which now snapped at its own back where a chunk of mud was affixed to the fur.

It hadn't done any damage, but it had most certainly distracted it.

"Baby steps," Dotty said and she grinned.

The idea came to her in a flash of inspiration, and she executed it before she had time to think. She imagined each paw, with its pads and claws, encased in thick mud that had frozen to stillness. When the image settled, she sent it out with a puff of breath that somehow seemed to take everything in her.

She thudded to her knees to the sounds of yells and snarls of confusion. Her eyes barely opened but when they did, the animals strained to free their feet from where they were frozen to the ground. With them immobilized, the guards made short work of them and shouted to each other all the while about what must have happened.

Vaguely, she was aware of someone who climbed beside her and lifted her down and, a little while later, of the jolting motion of a cart. She registered nothing more than the fact that she was safe and warm. Total exhaustion claimed her, and she slept.

"Whoa! Whoa. Whoa." Jacob stabbed furiously at the keys. "Whoa, fuck. Who put the limit on her powers?"

"I did." Nick stepped beside him. "Why?"

"Well, it's a good thing you did because she ran out of mana with a single spell and went through almost her entire life force as well. If it weren't for your one-HP hard stop, we'd have been able to test her heart on a character restart." He shuddered.

"What spell did she use?" Amber asked as she hurried toward them.

"Only the same Stone-Shock, but at multiple targets. It's supposed to be *realistic*," Jacob explained. "The idea is that, exactly like freediving farther than you should, you can overextend yourself with magic. With most people, it wouldn't happen because they would naturally pull back. She doesn't seem to have that instinct, and if Nick hadn't put that limit in place, things might have gotten bad there."

"I'm not sure that should be there," she said softly. "We need the data, Jacob." She had her arms wrapped around herself. "But…"

"But…" Nick echoed. He nodded. "Look, I think it makes sense to give her the regular rules later, but for now, when she's still getting used to it, let's give her an easy mode, all right?"

She nodded but continued to chew her lip.

"We're still getting useful data," Jacob told her. "Among other things, we're learning what various players do and don't consider dangerous."

"That's for sure," Amber said. "Ugh, why don't we keep beer around here? I need a drink."

CHAPTER ELEVEN

At midafternoon, Dotty woke with the sun peeking over the edge of the cart enough to shine in her eyes. She squinted and sat. A young dwarven man sat nearby, kicking his feet as he watched the caravan's slow progress, and she cleared her throat.

"What happened?"

He looked wordlessly at her, his eyes very round, then leapt off the cart without a word to her and ran off, shouting for Per.

That wasn't the best sign. She sighed as she waited for the other man. The leather harness above her robes hadn't chafed, but she could feel where the outlines of it had cut into her skin while she slept. It must have been hours.

Per appeared and hopped onto the back of the cart. "You're awake. Good. You seemed to only be tired and still somewhat alert, so we continued rather than sending you back with Warnulf."

"Is he the one who was hurt?" she asked.

"Yes." He shook his head. "But he knew what he signed up for. Protecting a caravan through these lands can be dangerous."

"I meant to talk to you about that." She remembered the stories from her youth and she also remembered what every hunter she knew had said. "That wasn't normal behavior for wolves."

Her companion looked at her, confused.

"Those wolves were well-fed," she said. "And well-fed, healthy wolves don't attack humans—people, I mean. They stay away from everyone."

Per shook his head. "Wolves are dangerous. I'm sure there's an explanation."

Dotty forbore to say that some of the explanations weren't so savory. For all she knew, after all, the beasts functioned differently in this world. If the person who programmed them hadn't known enough to make them docile, after all, maybe that was the whole explanation.

She held her tongue for now.

"We're grateful for your help," he told her. "I've never seen magic like that." He shrugged, embarrassed. "Well, I've never seen magic."

"No?" she asked, surprised.

"Are wizards common where you come from?" He looked astounded. "I can't imagine such a world. Imagine how powerful we would be if every guard in our caravan had your powers." He patted her hand. "You keep resting. We'll be at the campsite in no more than an hour, I should think."

Dotty sat in the cart as it jostled over the roads and let her mind drift. She wanted to get out and walk but she had exhausted all her energy when she cast the spell.

"Prima?" she murmured. "What happened when I attacked the wolves?"

"You used all your magic and proceeded to drain most of your life force. There appears to be a block that doesn't allow you to drain it entirely. Otherwise, you would have died."

She sat bolt upright. "What?"

"In the game. Not necessarily in your physical body."

"Not…*necessarily?*" she asked with a dangerous edge to her tone.

"*I don't have enough data to speculate further.*" A pause followed and she assumed the AI was thinking. "*It was not my intention to alarm you.*"

"How would I not be alarmed when you tell me I might have died?" Panic rose in her chest. "I didn't know I could cast a spell big enough to drain all my…*life.*"

"*You won't,*" Prima said. "*The block is there.*"

Dotty curled her arms around her knees and tried to focus. "I shouldn't be here. I don't know what I'm doing."

"*I thought that was how humans do most things.*" After another pause, she continued. "*Your facial expression suggests that you think I am mocking you. I am not. What I said was not intended as a joke.*"

She sniffled and felt four years old again. "I take it you haven't talked to many humans."

"*Not many, no.*"

Her mind recalled the years of children in diapers and siblings hitting each other with sticks, wide-eyed when they realized they had done harm. "You'll learn," she said. "Everyone does."

"*Okay.*"

They sat in silence until the caravan stopped and she clambered out of the cart to look around. The clearing in the trees where the snow barely covered the ground and the winds didn't touch as fully as they did beyond it would make a good camp.

"What needs doing?" she asked one of the nearby dwarves.

"Per said we were to let you rest, Zauberer," the young woman said respectfully.

"I'd much prefer to help." Dotty looked at her as imperiously as she could. "What tasks need to be done?"

The woman swallowed. "The tents need to be set up and fresh game caught for dinner if any can be found. A fire made—"

"I'll catch the game," she said. "Will you eat anything?"

"Yes, Zauberer."

She unsheathed one of the daggers from her belt and went hunting. Of course, she could use her magic but right now, she didn't feel ready to do that.

"You have to get back on the horse sometime, Dot," she muttered quietly.

But maybe not tonight.

In her youth, she'd been a good hand at setting snares, but there wasn't time for that before dinner. Instead, she tramped through the snow, ignored the feel of her robes getting sodden, and looked for the telltale tracks of rabbits and squirrels—or foxes, which might lead her to warrens.

She found the first rabbit huddled in the snow and the shadow it cast rendered it unusually visible. Dotty took care to walk away from it first as if she hadn't noticed it before she turned and threw her dagger by the point.

The idea had merit but unfortunately, she missed.

CLUMSY, Level 2, the screen read.

With a sigh, she plodded forward to retrieve her knife. She could hear the people at the camp still talking and she made sure to search beyond the clearing but remain reasonably close to the camp lest she lose herself in the woods.

Unfortunately, her boots were not made for snow.

It took her seven attempts and each one made her both more confident and more annoyed until she had a brace of rabbits to bring to the camp. When she appeared, bedraggled and with the creatures in both hands, people turned to stare at her. Fires were still being kindled, half the tents were up, and the cooks had only begun to search through their stores of preserved meat.

"I couldn't find any winter onions," Dotty said with as much dignity as she could muster. "Does anyone have a stool I could borrow while I skin these?"

No one spoke but someone hurried to get her a stool from one of the carts.

She sat and swore and occasionally scraped her cold hands,

but it wasn't long before the carcasses were skinned—she'd left the guts away from the camp—and turned on spits over the fires. Grimacing, she scrubbed her hands with snow and tucked them into one of the few dry places on her robes to warm them.

Per came to find her sometime later when she was hammering stakes into the ground for the tents. "I take it you're not one for resting," he said.

"I'm not," she agreed.

"Where does a wizard learn all of this?" he asked. He took the hammer and helped her pull up the frame of the tent.

"D'you think wizards are born in special mansions?" she asked him. "When I was little, even in some towns, you foraged for your food. We didn't churn our butter or grind flour, but we did most other things most of the time."

"And you don't mind doing it now?" he asked her.

Dotty gave him a grim smile. "My mother had a saying. You can tell much about a person by what they think of getting their hands dirty."

"I think I would like your mother," Per said after a moment of reflection. "Well, we have a saying in Berghold, too. The hunter gets the first cut of meat so I'll expect to hear no complaints when we serve you first." He wandered away, a twinkle in his eye, as she went into the tent and put her bedroll where she wanted it.

It was a good meal—the kind where there weren't seconds, and not because she wanted to watch her waistline. Instead, it was because there was no more food to be had and the day of exhaustion and the work of setting up camp made the food tastier than anything she could remember.

She went to bed in the only dry robes she had, glad for her trace of warmth and dinner—and even, as she fell asleep, for her taste of adventure.

"Dotty?" Prima asked when she was almost unconscious.

"Mm-hmm?"

"Sleep well."

CHAPTER TWELVE

Dotty slept very well, indeed. She awoke to the first rays of sunlight filtering through the tent flap, the quiet snoring of her two tent-mates, and the sounds of the camp waking up. With a smile, she sat quickly, reveling in the feeling of exhausted muscles—not a feeling one had very often in old age—and dressed in her now dry robes and armor.

She slipped outside as quietly as she could to join the others who were already up and about. The leftover scraps of rabbit from the night before had been simmering with potatoes and barley for a hearty stew that would carry them through the day. When she took her first mouthful, she noticed a definite kick of beer in the taste and caught a wink from the cook.

"Everyone knows a good ale will keep ye warm," the woman said.

With the chill in the air, she couldn't disagree and simply grinned in response and ate hungrily. A generous bowl left her feeling contented and almost sleepy enough to return to her bedroll, but she knew better than to let herself lie down. There was work to be done in the chill morning air. With her breath puffing and the rich purple of her cloak catching her eye from time to time, she helped to take down some of the first shelters and checked the snares the hunters had set overnight.

Two more rabbits and a squirrel were the results of their efforts. It wasn't much for an entire camp, but she would keep an eye out during the day. She gutted them, hung them on one of the carts, and cleaned her hands, and she had barely glanced at the blue of the sky when one of the sentries called a warning.

Everyone scrambled for their weapons at once. Dwarves tumbled out of their tents, still in their smallclothes but with their weapons at the ready. Everyone's attention fixed in the direction of the call.

As they listened, however, a shouted conversation could be heard—a call and answer, a passcode. Per sheathed his short-sword, set off around the bend of the road, and returned only a few minutes later with a messenger leading a tired horse.

Whatever news had come from Berghold, it didn't look good. The leader disappeared into his tent with the messenger, only to poke his head out a moment later and gesture at Dotty.

"You, come listen to this. The rest of you, pack up camp—double-time."

Everyone scurried to obey. She went curiously into the main tent and found a familiar face under the messenger's helmet.

"Lyle!"

"The same." He gave a rakish bow and clasped her hand. "How's the journey been so far?"

"Not good," the leader said bluntly. "Although at least we know why now." He was seated at a makeshift desk and pored over a letter composed of dwarven runes. He looked up at her, and she was surprised to see little warmth in his face. "Tell me, Zauberer Hunt—is there any truth to the charges in this letter?"

The words made no sense for a long moment. She tilted her head to the side and frowned at him.

Finally, it snapped into place.

The letter was about her. Someone had accused her of something and it had to do with the attack on the caravan. She went hot, then cold, and couldn't tell if what she felt was dread or fury. Either way, it certainly seemed set to expand to fill her entire chest.

"I don't know what the letter says," she said as calmly as she could, "but I had nothing to do with the attack on the caravan yesterday. I have not and would not endanger any of the artifacts or those guarding them."

Per stared at her, his gaze hard, and she responded in kind.

Unexpectedly, it was Lyle who broke the silence by laughing uproariously. He dropped into a chair and propped one booted foot on the other. "Since I know who sent the message, I think I can guess what it says. There's *grave danger*"—he waved his hands to articulate the words "—from a sinister outside force, which he is *of course* too well-bred to put a name to. But it is *almost certainly* the new wizard, although again, he can truthfully say he never *actually suggested that*." To her, he added, "The message was sent from none other than Councilor Marwitz. When I saw who sent it, I decided to deliver it and see how you were doing. It appears I chose the right time to appear. Come, now, Per. You can't truly believe she's behind some dark plot?"

Per leaned back in his chair and looked thoughtfully at her. "Truly? I don't know what to believe. I know she's done good work to ingratiate herself. We were attacked yesterday by wolves—"

"Something you weren't worried about," Dotty said, annoyed, "even when I pointed out that they didn't behave like any wolves I'd seen before."

He didn't respond to that. "She did point that out," he said to Lyle, "but she also went out of her way to be a model part of the caravan. Not only did she defeat the wolves, she hunted food for dinner and helped set up camp. Who's to say this wasn't merely part of a plot to gain our trust so she could divert us to another road?"

She now saw he was terrified of her. He was afraid that if he challenged her, she would kill him. That should make her feel sorry for him but instead, it only made her angry.

"Are you kidding me?" The words exploded from her. "I helped you so I'm suspicious? If I hadn't helped you, wouldn't I be suspicious too? So there's no winning for me. I thought when I came here, I wouldn't have to deal with these things."

Per looked less worried now—after all, she wasn't throwing fireballs—but he still hadn't relaxed. "What am I supposed to think?" he asked. "Everyone in this caravan is known to me except you. Our families have held Berghold together for generations. Now, as attacks befall our caravan, I receive good information telling me there's a plot against it—and that someone in our ranks might be planning to betray us. I ask you, Zauberer, what would you think?"

"I'd ask yourself why you had guards in the first place," she said tartly. "Clearly, you've needed to protect the caravan before. Not only that, but the people of this world know that every year you send artifacts of inestimable value to Insea. Maybe there is a plot this year, but it wouldn't be anything new, would it?"

He chewed his lip. "I have to admit you have a point."

"Of course she does," Lyle said.

"And who's to say this councilor has anything more than worry to go on?" Dotty asked.

To her surprise, both her companions shook their heads.

"The councilor would never lie about such a thing," Per said.

Even Lyle, for all his dislike, seemed to agree. "Per is right. Marwitz is liable to jump to conclusions about who our enemies are, but he wouldn't lie outright about having information. If he says there's a plot, then there's a plot."

"Great," she muttered. She had mostly enjoyed the realism of the game thus far but in her opinion, having to work with people she despised took the realism a little too far.

Per looked at Lyle. "Even with this information, do you swear that you support Zauberer Hunt?"

"I swear," Lyle said promptly. "She is known to my family and her loyalty was assured by a man to whom I owe my life many times over."

The leader sighed and nodded. "I apologize," he told her, "but after almost trusting you enough to show you the runes of Berghold's creation, I found it too easy to believe that I might simply be a fool."

"No offense taken," Dotty said tightly. The words weren't true but her lifelong habit of politeness wasn't easily broken.

When Per left, Lyle sighed and looked at her.

"I have nothing to do with any plot," she said fiercely.

"I never thought ye did," he assured her. "But for all ye weren't born here, ye sure take a slight to yer honor the same way as any dwarf I've ever met."

She managed a laugh and after a pause, she admitted, "I almost killed myself protecting the caravan."

Lyle looked worried. He had been in the process of taking a book out of his bag, but now he paused. "What happened?"

"I made the spell too big." She clenched her hands. "I'm afraid of the magic now. What if I go too far again?"

He sighed and took the book out. It was heavy and bound in leather with gilt runes on the cover. "Justin appeared again to give ye this book—he just missed the caravan, so I'd already planned to come give this to ye. It's a book of new spells."

Dotty shook her head. "I'm…not sure I trust myself."

"Ye need a teacher," he said.

"And in the meantime, I'll pay my way on the caravan another way," she agreed.

"Surely ye can still study—"

"No." Her voice was fierce. "I'll learn to fight with weapons. I'm not a bad hand at throwing a knife or using a bow. I bet I could fight with a staff."

Lyle gave her a considering look. "Well, if that's what ye want —but ye keep the book. It's Justin's wishes and I'll not gainsay him. And I'll stay to help ye learn weapons."

She hesitated, nodded, but frowned quickly. "Who d'you think is behind the attacks?"

"Hell if I know," Lyle said. "It could be anyone, but if they sent wolves, it means they have magic of some kind." He stroked his beard thoughtfully. "I'll send a message to Zaara. She might know if there's a wizard who dabbles in this kind of thing."

Dotty nodded and caught a flicker of motion out of the corner of her eye, where a shadow moved away from the wall of the tent.

So Per had stayed to listen. The tricky bastard. Despite herself, she hoped he hadn't organized the attacks. He seemed to view the world as fairly as he could and she'd be sad to know he was a traitor.

She sighed. "Well, we'd best get the camp packed up. We have another day of riding ahead of us."

"And training," Lyle added, "apparently."

CHAPTER THIRTEEN

"I simply don't understand *why*," Dotty said a few days later. "If it's proper form to keep the dagger facing this way, why do I need to learn how to switch it the other way?"

Lyle, who was showing her how to change her weapons from a forward to a backward grip, fixed her with a glare. "So ye can be adaptable," he said as if it were self-explanatory. "The point needs to go into yer opponent and ye can't always get there with a forward grip."

She grimaced and tried to focus. He had seized the lunch break for practice and had announced that neither of them would eat until she had the grip-switch mastered to his liking. Her rations sat temptingly out of reach—a little apple, streaked red and green, a dense oatcake, a thick sliver of meat, and a slice of sharp cheese.

Back in the day, she would not have considered that a meal. Right now, after a morning of walking and without a bag of chips in sight, she couldn't imagine anything more heavenly.

Lyle saw her longing look. "The sooner ye master this," he said, "the sooner we *both* eat. And let me tell ye, missy, I do not like the idea of waitin' much longer."

She rolled her eyes and it surprised her into laughter.

"What's so funny?" he asked suspiciously.

Dotty shook her head and her lips twitched madly. She didn't know how to tell him that it had been a very long time since anyone had called her "missy." Or, for that matter, since she hadn't been filled with the unconscious but pervasive awareness of her weakening body or learned something new like this dagger trick.

More to the point, it was utterly hilarious that simply being called "missy" had activated her eye-rolling, teenaged self.

Lyle wouldn't understand any of that. Still snickering inwardly, she returned to the exercise. The switch from forward to back could be done in at least two ways. First, with a little upward throw in addition to the flip to keep the dagger in relatively the same place above the ground. Second, by moving both dagger and hand in a smooth, concerted motion so the hilt rolled over the palm.

The second one looked much more elegant, and she had to admit that she wanted to be able to do it.

Nevertheless, five disastrous attempts later, she had to concede that…what was the polite way to say it?

She was entirely hopeless at the skill.

Prima had less diplomatic opinions. *"Who needs someone to attack the caravan when you're inside it?"*

"Oh, shut up," Dotty muttered.

"No, no, I think it's hilarious that Per was right. You will destroy the caravan from inside. You're merely doing it by sheer incompetence."

"For the love of—" She directed a glare skyward. "I won't kill anyone."

"Are you sure about that?"

Grimly, she rolled her eyes again and decided she'd have to do it the uncool way. She blew her breath out in annoyance, focused on the two daggers, and cleared her mind entirely before she gave each one the requisite lift and flip and moved her hands around them in midair to grasp them backward.

"Ha!" Lyle said.

Startled, she opened her eyes. Both weapons were held in a strong grip and facing the desired way. She'd caught one finger on a blade while she did the switch and bright spots of blood dripped into the snow, but between the cold air and her pleasure at doing the switch correctly, she could barely feel the pain.

"Ha!" she echoed.

He grinned at her. "Five more times an' ye can have lunch."

Now that she had done it once, she fumbled far less. Dotty repeated the trick perfectly twice before she attempted to speed up and both daggers twirled away to land in the snow. She waded after them, swearing under her breath, and repeated the trick three more times at normal speed.

When she looked up, Lyle was smiling and seemed pleased—and held her lunch out to her.

"Good job," he told her.

"I don't know what's so good about it." She ignored the lunch and picked the daggers up.

"Ah, ye didn't even notice, did ye?" He pointed to the back of a nearby cart. "Sheathe those daggers for now an' go sit. We'll eat while the caravan sets out."

She scrambled onto the back of the cart—this kind of mobility was still wondrous to her—and dug into her lunch as the caravan set off. She looked curiously at Lyle and he grinned around a mouthful of jerky.

"When ye started into the five repetitions, ye were tryin' t' do it—by the time ye finished, ye were tryin' t' do it faster. That's an important change, ye know."

Dotty considered this as she chewed. He was right. She had started that set of five repetitions with the simple satisfaction that she could do the trick at all. By the time she finished, however, she already felt confident enough to be dissatisfied with her level of skill.

"Now comes the hard part," Lyle told her.

She swallowed a mouthful of food hastily. "Wait, what?"

"For every hour ye practice, ye get better, eh?" He licked his fingers and took a deep drink from his waterskin. "But the amount ye get better gets smaller an' smaller. That was the part I always hated."

"Not me." She smiled and shook her head. "It's the part where I can't even begin to do it that I hate. The repetition and training —now, *that*, I like."

He looked at her with new appreciation. "Well, then, ye should take well t' being a warrior…or a wizard."

Dotty shook her head emphatically. They had argued about this every day until she had begun to fantasize about planting his head in the snow and jumping up and down on it.

"I may not know anythin' about magic—" he began and she seized on that.

"You're right. You don't. Neither do I."

"I may not know anything about magic," he repeated mean-ingfully, "but I do know one or two things about fighting a battle, and some o' those things come from fighting with Justin, who's not only a melee fighter but a wizard as well."

She harrumphed. "You keep trying to convince me and it keeps not working."

"An' I keep trying because there's at least one thing I know about ye on short acquaintance." Lyle fixed her with another glare. "An' it's that ye hate failing at anythin'."

A dramatic silence settled over them. Dotty knew her face had shown the depth of her reaction and it was too late to pretend that Lyle was wrong.

In fact, he was very, very right. There was nothing in the world she hated more than to fail at something. It was what had kept her going in school through the classes she hated, and it was what kept her going when she tried to raise children or fix a stubborn piece of plumbing or make sense of her taxes after Harry died. She *hated* failing.

"So, if I were ye," he said smugly, "I would give thought to the next way ye plan t' learn magic because ye'll not rest properly until ye've cracked it."

He hopped off the back of the cart, whistling, and headed off, calling to one of the younger guards about hunting more rabbits.

Alone again, she sat and stared at the pack that held the book of spells.

"Here's something interesting," Jacob said. He stared at a set of printouts he held as he walked to Amber and Nick. "Guys? If you have a second—" He broke off when he saw their lack of response was due not to their focus on something else but instead, the fact that both of them had mouthfuls of blintzes.

He narrowed his eyes at them. They returned his stare, completely still as if he were a T-Rex that wouldn't be able to see them unless they moved.

"So, what you're telling me," he said conversationally, "is that I have one coworker who eats nothing but popcorn, and now I have two others who eat nothing but cheese blintzes."

Nick swallowed his mouthful. "And coffee," he said as if that solved the problem entirely.

Amber nodded and looked vindicated.

Jacob glared at them. "We are in a city that is full of every kind of food imaginable," he told them severely. "We are getting something else for lunch today." He cleared his throat. "Now, as I was saying..."

His partners grumbled but gathered around the printouts as he spread them over the desk.

A pause followed as they studied the data.

"When was the baseline taken?" she asked finally.

"It's a composite of the first day she came to talk to us, two samples taken during the two weeks before she entered the game, as well as the first day she was in the game."

She chewed her lip. The numbers they looked at suggested that Dorothy's stress levels had steadily diminished and that the decrease had been matched by a corresponding increase in her happiness.

"It's not conclusive on its own," Jacob said, "I know that. But she's learning new things, she's not in pain all the time—"

"So…you think we should check the progress of the cancer?" Nick asked. "The research about mood and disease is fairly divisive."

"No," he said, surprised. "No, that's not what I meant at all. I mean—" He stopped, a little startled because he genuinely hadn't considered the idea that Dotty's improved mood would result in the cancer leaving her body. "Huh. No, we should explore that. I only meant that she seems undeniably happier since she went into the game. I think that's something we should focus on."

"Because…" the other man prompted.

He looked at the two of them and fought the urge to shake them by the shoulders and shriek. "*Because*," he said through gritted teeth, "it is good when people are happy. That's it. That's all. She has a much better quality of life now. That is good."

He restrained himself from further comment during the long moment of silence that followed.

"Oh," Amber said. She sounded completely blindsided. "Oh, I hadn't thought of that."

"You don't say." Jacob left the printouts where they were. "Look, I'm not saying the best option is for everyone in the world to escape into some kind of alternate life. I'm only saying that if some people who are in chronic pain could have this option, it would be cool. She's learning things, she's adventuring, and she has the chance to do things she could never do at this point in her life. It's not like she could physically tromp through the mountains."

His partners nodded.

"It's funny," she said after a moment. "I have all those thoughts in my head—people shouldn't escape the real world, it's not healthy—but why? Why *shouldn't* they be happy and free of pain in situations like this? Why *shouldn't* they go exploring? What's different between exploring Berghold and exploring...uh, Prague?" She took a sip of coffee. "Huh," she said and wandered away.

"Maybe that's what we tell her daughter," Nick suggested. "Show her how happy her mother is."

"Even if we could simply send her Dorothy's medical records —which we absolutely cannot—I'm not sure this would make her feel better," Jacob pointed out. "We should keep thinking. In the meantime...well, this is interesting, that's all."

CHAPTER FOURTEEN

The caravan emerged from the shadow of the mountains partway through the afternoon. Dotty, who had never much liked winter, was surprisingly sad to see the snow gradually give way to bare rock and scrub brush. There had been something peaceful about the snowy stillness and the chill air, something that kept the blood pumping.

Well, in a manner of speaking. She wondered if her body did all the same shivering.

That thought was absorbing enough to make her walk directly into the back of a stopped cart. She rubbed her forehead, glared at the cart, and hoped no one had seen her—although the faint snickering in the back of her mind told her that Prima, at least, had noticed everything.

The land they were in now was high plains, the kind of vista she pictured Montana looking like—or maybe Mongolia. With the mountains behind and miles of tall, wavy grasses in every direction, she could see more sky than she had ever imagined.

It was probably the openness and desolation of the plains that made the attack so unexpected.

One moment, all of them were walking while carts jostled on

the dirt road, accompanied by snatches of dwarven song drifting on the breeze. In the next, arrows whistled ominously and horses screamed. One of the drivers fell from her seat with a cry of pain, her fingers clutched over a spreading patch of crimson on her sleeve. Dotty looked around wildly for the source of the onslaught.

The grass around them waved wildly now as their attackers ran through it.

Arrows, she thought. This wasn't wolves or buffalo or anything even arguably natural. This was people—and maybe she had a chance to learn who was really behind this.

That galvanized her. She drew her daggers and tried to decide what, exactly, she should do first. The guards fanned out around the caravan with their weapons drawn, but without a clear line of sight to their opponents and with their fear of the arrows, they didn't seem particularly sure of themselves.

Dotty, who had been at the end of the caravan, scanned the grass around her. On her right, the attackers were closing in faster. Very slowly and quietly, she stepped into the grass away from the wagons.

When the enemy burst out of cover, she was ready. The archers had taken the back of the line, ready to cut down anyone who tried to run, but they hadn't bargained on having someone at their back. She slunk out of the grass and stabbed with all her might at the exposed back of one of the archers.

The leather and bone under the blade offered resistance, but it was no match for her strike. The man uttered a terrible scream and fell as blood welled from the wound.

Her mouth dropped open in horror, but the others turned toward her now and she had no time to think. She recalled her mother telling her once—very seriously—that you only had to be nice if people hadn't attacked you first. "As soon as someone hits you, you can hit right back. Don't worry about being ladylike." The remembered words strengthened her resolve.

These people had attacked first and they fully intended to kill everyone in the caravan.

She launched herself into action with a yell of fury. The truth was that she didn't want to do this, but she channeled her fury directly at her opponents. One of the archers stumbled and raised his bow, and she batted it aside with one arm before she thrust her blade into his stomach.

Behind her, the first man she'd stabbed shouted as he struggled to his feet and stumbled toward her with hatred in his eyes. He knew he was dying and he planned to repay the favor.

While she knew she could turn and stab him, she'd leave the others at her exposed back. With a flash of inspiration, she flipped her right dagger to a backward grip before she sank into a crouch and drove it back. The man fell with a choking cry.

"Okay, Dotty," she muttered belligerently. "Lesson learned. Make sure they're dead before you turn your back."

She had no more time to think, however, as she whirled, slashed, dodged, and ducked. Every time she cut an enemy down, another took their place. Cuts burned like lines of fire along her arms and back, painful reminders of where she had failed to protect herself. From the yells of her adversaries, they hadn't expected her to wield daggers and hurl herself into battle.

It took a moment for her to realize that her robes marked her as a wizard and another to realize that they didn't offer half the protection of armor. If she'd worn full leather plating like the other guards, the wounds that had opened on her skin wouldn't be there.

There was nothing to be done about it now, though.

A shout caught her attention and Dotty looked hastily to where Per was surrounded by marauders.

Thought was a luxury she had no time for. She sprinted to him, her muscles working hard. One of the bars at the top of her vision—the red one—was about half-empty, but the way she saw it, she had two choices. She could either slink away to heal herself and run the risk of her enemies finding her, or she could eliminate them before they could do more damage.

And if she wanted to save Per, there was no choice at all.

She narrowed her focus and pounded sideways into one of the attackers, but proceeded to trip over his now prone form.

"It would seem someone should have taught you how to tackle properly," Prima said.

"Is there"—her breath came in gasps as she pushed to her feet and snatched her daggers up—"a right way to do that?"

"No, of course not. That's why absolutely anyone can be a linebacker."

"Fine, fine, you've made your point." Dotty rolled her eyes as she dispatched the enemy she'd upended into the grass. Bile rose in her throat, no matter how much she told herself that this wasn't real.

It was both more difficult than she'd ever expected and far easier—and she was very much afraid that it wasn't merely easy because she knew none of this was real.

She was afraid that, deep down, the violence came naturally.

On the plus side, a battle didn't allow much time for introspection. Three marauders were left and two of them had decided to focus on her—probably a good choice on their part, given that Per didn't look like he was doing too well.

Dotty slashed at them but they carried short swords instead of daggers and were able to dance out of her range.

Which meant she wouldn't be able to defeat them in time to help Per.

Resolutely, she turned her back on them. She knew how stupid it was but saw no other option and charged Per's attacker. The woman fell with a heavy thud and a quickly silenced cry of pain, and Dotty snatched her short sword. At her side, Per sank to his knees.

The best thing she could do for him was end this quickly. She dropped both her daggers in front of him and took a second short-sword from his limp fingers.

"Keep your wits about you," she told him urgently. "Stay with me."

Without listening for a response, she lunged at the remaining two attackers.

Whatever they expected, it was not a woman in mage robes who wielded two short swords like daggers. Their eyes widened and they scattered in an attempt to force her to focus on one and leave her back unguarded.

Dotty yelled for help, barreled toward one of them, and left the other scrambling to catch up with her. If they could play her like a fiddle by having two of them, her only chance was to remove one of them from the equation.

She learned the hard way that two short swords could do significant damage and was covered in blood and a little shell-shocked when the second one came within range.

Her response was not what he expected. Rather than attack, she threw up on him. It wasn't what she intended to do and she was far too horrified to enjoy the look of surprise on his face, but at least it surprised him enough that he didn't kill her on the spot. She wiped her mouth with the back of one hand, took a breath, and stabbed him through the chest with all her might. When he sank to his knees and slumped onto his side, she looked up.

The rest of the caravan stared at her, open-mouthed.

The screen abruptly filled with scrolling text. **SHORT SWORDS, Level 1; SHORT SWORDS, Level 2; SHORT SWORDS, Level 3; HILT FLIP, Level 4, SHORT SWORDS, Level 4.**

Dotty's head was buzzing and her health bar was almost three quarters gone. She stumbled to Per and sank beside him. A patch of red spread from one shoulder and she pressed a wad of her skirt over it awkwardly. "I need a…I need a—"

One of the caravan's healers ran closer. "I've got it."

"Good." She stood and immediately sat again, unable to maintain her balance. The buzzing in her ears was louder and she had begun to see spots. "Prima…"

"You're okay," the AI told her soothingly. *"There are no more attackers and you will begin regaining health now. That said…"*

"Yes?" Dotty murmured.

Lyle finished the sentence for Prima. "Ye're lucky ye fight like a berserker," he told her bluntly as he came to help her stand. He looped one of her arms over his shoulder and eased her back to sit on a stool someone had pulled off a cart before he looked gravely at her. "Because ye haven't got the armor for this," he finished. "If ye want t' fight with daggers, we need to get ye new gear."

She was dimly aware of her robes being ripped and bandages being applied, as well as a salve that smelled spicy and felt like the burn of sticking your hand directly into a pile of ice. She flinched, but strong hands held her in place as the healers worked and her health bar began to climb quickly.

Someone pressed a flask into her hand and she took a sip. The burn of the brandy helped to ground her. She handed it back and looked at Lyle. "Is Per all right? Did we lose anyone?"

He had to look around before he could answer her, which she hated. The battle had been pitched enough, then, that he was worried. At length, he shook his head.

"I don't see any of ours dead. But that's not so much a surprise —these are some o' the best guards in Berghold." He nodded toward the front of the caravan. "An' they got to Per in time thanks to you."

Dotty looked at him and her eyes filled with tears. She sniffed and looked away, ashamed.

"Ye've only killed animals before," he guessed. "Animals for meat or the ones attacking livestock."

She nodded and didn't trust her voice.

"It'll get easier," Lyle told her bluntly. "But not everyone takes to it. The only thing I'd say is if ye ever do become a wizard, remember that even if you don't feel the blow strike home and get their blood on ye, they're equally as dead."

Dotty couldn't bring herself to nod. She looked at her hands and after a moment, he wandered away and left her in peace.

"Are you all right?" Prima asked her.

"I don't know," she said honestly. "When I thought of adventuring, I didn't think it would be like this."

The AI said nothing for a long time. Finally, she said, *"They're wondering whether they should take you out of the game, you know."*

Her head jerked up. "No."

"No?"

"No." She stared at the sky, the grass, and the bodies. "I lived my whole life never seeing the parts like this, but they happened even in real life. I won't run away simply because this is unpleasant. I won't go back to a safe little world where nothing like this happens in front of me. I'll see it and see it through."

CHAPTER FIFTEEN

Surprisingly, the caravan got underway shortly after the attack. The marauders' bodies were laid out with businesslike efficiency at the side of the road, although stripped of their weapons.

"We'll not take the time to bury them," one of the dwarven guards said, "but there's no call to leave them without rites."

She stared at him. "You're saying funeral rites for them?"

A few of the guards looked at her as though she were a heartless monster.

"Yes," the one she was speaking to said. "After every battle, one says rites for those one killed."

Dotty, who very much doubted that the attackers would have given them the same courtesy, nevertheless held her tongue and nodded. She stood respectfully while rites were said—even Per, pale and barely upright, was there—and murmured a few words under her breath. They weren't genuine perhaps but they were the right kind of words.

Lyle came to walk with her when they resumed the journey once more, although he didn't speak, for which she was grateful.

Instead, in silence, he showed her how to clean her weapons while she walked.

It wasn't the easiest thing she had ever done. Holding the daggers and short swords reminded her of how it had felt to plunge them into the enemy. They were sharp implements and beautifully made, but she had thought of them as cooking knives —something her first uses of them had only reinforced.

It felt very different to have killed people with them.

The wagons and carts turned right at one of the branches in the road and she followed without thinking about it. She only noticed that something was different when the other dwarves began to murmur and the news spread from the front to the back of the caravan about where they were going.

Presumably because she was an outsider, no one thought to inform her. She wasn't quite sure where they were in any case and simply accepted that Lyle would look more worried than he presently did if something was wrong. After a while, he joined the front ranks of guards and left her to her thoughts.

The plains were beautiful but in time, they became incredibly boring. The occasional sight of a bird wheeling on the high currents of wind was the most excitement she could find. Not only that, her feet ached and she was exhausted. She could see little red numbers trailing away every once in a while as her stamina wore down, but the process was slow enough that she estimated she could walk until nightfall without any major problem.

It was easy to lose track of time, so she wasn't sure how long it had been before a town appeared in the distance.

Dotty pushed through the group until she found Lyle. "Where are we?"

"Only a little nowhere town." His face was unusually expressionless.

"And do we get to stay here tonight?" She was so happy at the thought of a real bed that she could have cried. "I don't know how to get money but I'll pay anything for a chance to have a hot meal and some sleep."

He relaxed somewhat. "If we stay here tonight, I'll make sure you get a bed in the inn—and none of us will say no to a hot meal if the town has a place that'll serve us. They probably get most of their trade from caravans, though, so I'd guess they'll have some-place for us."

She smiled. Even the thought of a hot meal put a little spring in her step.

"We'll also," he said, "get you proper armor."

"Oh, good." She raised an eyebrow. "You won't argue with me about magic again?"

"No." Lyle said. The word hung in the air for a while until he added, "But Justin sent me with that book and I'll be damned if I'll let you get away without reading it. Whether we stay the night or not, you'll spend time reading tonight."

Dotty grumbled, but she knew better than to press her luck. He was certainly stubborn enough to make her life miserable if she didn't at least make the effort.

Besides, her brief foray into melee combat had shown her it wasn't necessarily safer than magic.

The caravan hadn't even stopped before he whisked her away to procure new armor. It was strange to see dwarven-style build-ings out in the open air instead of underground in Berghold, but a group of them called these plains home. Only a few houses had the taller profile of human dwellings, and most of the people she saw were her height.

The town was, indeed, quite small—or narrow, rather. It stretched along the road and most houses displayed a sign out front for a shop of some kind, while many had stables attached. As Lyle had said, most of their custom came from the caravans and they were prepared to take care of travelers—from spare beds, to stables, to bales of hay for the horses.

The leatherworker was located on the far edge of town, something that seemed unfair in light of her aching feet but made more sense as soon as she smelled the site.

Dotty decided to breathe through her mouth for the foreseeable future.

She was shy at the thought of taking her tattered robes off in front of a stranger, but the woman who took her measurements had no time for such qualms. She whisked her into the back and had her leather harness and robes off before she truly had time to protest. When she tried to fold her arms over her chest, the woman pulled one out straight to measure it with a harrumph.

"How d'ye plan to move in yer armor if I can't measure it, hmm?"

"She's right," Prima commented. *"Besides which, that isn't even your body."*

Swallowing a sharp rejoinder, she rolled her eyes and said nothing.

"And didn't you say that your goal was to be ugly here?"

Dotty was fairly sure there was a joke coming and she wasn't sure she wanted to know what it was. She looked at the sky, not wanting to mutter to the AI and have the leatherworker think she was loony. It was only when the woman left to get trial garments that she said, "Yes. I did say that."

"Good," Prima said promptly, *"because I've seen what she's choosing for you and let me tell you, it's not all that pretty.*

She snickered and went silent, leaving her to sigh and wonder who thought it was a good idea to give computers awareness.

Before the armor, she was given a linen tunic and pants to put on so that the protective items wouldn't chafe. "Given," of course, was a relative term—the woman threw the clothes over the wall of the changing room without a word.

"I'll need time to make the first alterations," she called. "Put those on while ye wait."

Dotty dressed and folded the tattered remnants of her robes. There wasn't much left that even vaguely resembled the elegant, comfortable garments. The best she could do with it, probably, was turn it into bandages.

She went out to wait with Lyle, who had returned with two brimming mugs of ale as well as the book. He patted a chair beside him and gave her the kind of smile she had usually seen on steely-eyed southern matriarchs.

Wordlessly, she sat. She knew better than to disobey that particular look.

With her ale in one hand, she began to peruse the book. The script was in runes but Prima showed her a translation superimposed above it in glowing white letters. Without meaning to, she fell into reading so intently that the sounds of the shop faded away.

The powers of the earth are those that span the heat of the forge, the pressure of a hammer, the tumbling fury of an avalanche, the life-giving richness of the soil...

The words drew her in and as she read, she was astounded at what she had summoned in the first attack on the caravan. Mud, after all, was not only earth but also water, and she learned that the sight of hardened earth encasing the wolves' feet was not so much the reality of the spell as an illusion. She had summoned the essence of the mud—the heaviness, the way it clung to the creatures' fur, and how it broke apart like a stone shattering beneath a pick-ax.

She could learn almost anything she wanted if she continued to work with earth magic. From the hot, quick flows of lava and the explosive power of a volcano—a force she was admonished *never* to summon without a large group of magic-users and extensive training—to the simple, homey magic of healing herb plants and weaving strength into poultices. Earth magic was broader than she had ever imagined it could be.

Dotty was almost disappointed when Lyle shook her out of her trance. He nodded to where the leatherworker waited, a suit of armor in her hands, and she made sure not to meet his gaze as she set the book down.

He looked *insufferably* smug.

The armor, to her surprise, fit almost perfectly. It was a rich, chestnut brown with brilliant red tooling at the edges of some of the panels. She could almost imagine that she was a lean, tall, elven huntress—until she remembered she was short and hadn't exactly watched her figure.

"This was what you came here to do, Dotty," she muttered quietly.

Still, there was something about wearing leather pants that made you wish you hadn't eaten quite so many helpings of mashed potatoes. It took almost all her courage to return to the main room.

Lyle looked at her and nodded in satisfaction. "Now, that'll protect ye a good sight better. Ready fer dinner?"

"Yes," Dotty said. She patted her stomach. "Although this doesn't have as much give in it as the robes did."

"Don't worry," the leatherworker advised her, "it'll get supple as ye wear it. No self-respectin' dwarf would make armor that couldn't fit through a good meal."

She smiled and waited while Lyle paid the woman. Once they were out in the sunshine, she asked, "When will I have money of my own? Are you keeping track of what I owe?"

"Justin gave me quite a princely sum for you," he said, thought for a moment, and dug into his purse to withdraw another, smaller leather packet. "I suppose ye might as well keep it yerself."

"Thank you." She stared at it. "How do I...earn more?"

"If ye run out of that, I'll be surprised." He scratched his chin. "Still, I know what it's like to not want charity. Tell ye what— when we're done with the meal, I'll show you the place where villagers post requests. We'll see if ye can make one or two coppers of yer own."

"I'd like that," she said happily.

CHAPTER SIXTEEN

Dinner was surprisingly good. Light, fluffy rolls studded with raisins and a rich bean soup with pieces of smoked ham were accompanied by flagon after flagon of delightful beer. Almost every dwarf, Dotty began to realize, brewed their own beer and was intensely proud of it. Each innkeeper extolled the virtues of theirs, and it was practically compulsory for travelers to compliment their host.

The members of the caravan ate heartily and traded stories, and she laughed at some of the antics of the younger ones. It turned out that while Per's generation snuck out into the mountains as a rite of teenage rebellion, the younger generations preferred to rappel down the sides of the Temple and climb the columns.

She contributed with cow-tipping.

Toward the end of the meal, Lyle went to speak to Per, who still looked pale and tired. His wounds hadn't healed yet, she thought, but there must have been magic worked or he wouldn't be seated with all of them and eating heartily.

The two dwarves held a whispered conversation and Lyle nodded a few times before he went to speak to a few of the other guards. Two of them accompanied him to the table, and he smiled at her.

"Per doesn't want anyone going out in ones and twos, not with someone stalking the caravan."

Dotty nodded and stood, hoping there would be a reasonable walk to wherever their destination was. She wasn't in any shape to fight for the next few minutes, not after so many helpings of bean soup. Cautious but excited, she followed him to a wall with scraps of parchment and notes scribbled in charcoal and perused them.

"Fight wolves? I suppose we've done that before." She tugged absentmindedly at one of the panels of her armor.

Lyle looked dubious. "Maybe. Last time I was hired to fight wolves, though, they turned out to be *werewolves*. It was quite a shock."

She replaced the piece of paper hastily. After the day she'd had, she wasn't in any mood to kill *people* and she didn't know what kind of unusual powers a werewolf would have.

Likewise, she skipped the bounty for a bear—she had no illusions about her ability to kill something that large—and the one on a band of thieves that seemed to be stealing bales of hay. Lyle frowned at that one before he tapped a scribbled note about nettles.

"I don't want to go around killing people," Dotty said, "but I'm not sure I want to spend my time weeding, either."

One of the guards laughed. He had gingery hair and blue-gray eyes, with a bright smile that was mostly obscured by his bushy beard. "No, they want the nettles for medicine. My da swore by it for hay fever."

"Mine used it for wounds that had gone rank," the other said. Tall by dwarven standards and a little older than his fellow guard, he had brown hair that was curly and almost black, and he wore his beard shorter than the others. She wondered if he was half-human but wasn't sure if that was a permissible question to ask.

In any case, she had other concerns.

"Good, so...very prickly plants that treat...various things. Also, I still think this is weeding." Dotty shrugged. "But I suppose we might as well keep an eye out—and we can hunt for rabbits at the same time."

The others agreed and they set off with her following the others' lead. A short distance outside the town, a smattering of trees appeared, the first signs of the true forest she thought she could see as a dark line on the horizon.

"The innkeeper said there's a stream to the west," the guard with curly hair told them. "Nettles grow in moist soil, yes? With some shade. So if we find a stand of trees near the water, that might be our spot."

The others agreed, and Dotty—still grumpy that she'd come into a fantasy world and was now doing yard work—followed while she flipped her daggers from a forward grip to a backward one and back again. She still couldn't roll the pommel over her palm without dropping it, and after the first time she almost lost it in the grass, she decided to stop trying.

The vegetation around them hummed with tiny insects and the scurrying of little animals. Every once in a while, a hawk shrieked, and she relaxed into the silence. In her youth, she had spent a few summers on her aunt's farm. When she was younger, she had hated those months and had yearned to be back in the city with her friends.

What she wouldn't give now for spare time to go running through the woods, finding streams and rabbit warrens—

She realized that was exactly what she was doing and snickered quietly. If it wasn't precisely human nature to complain about something and long for the same thing all at once, she didn't know what was.

Dotty scanned the ground every few steps to check for droppings and not far from the stand of trees, she saw the small, round rabbit pellets. She sheathed one dagger and held the other ready as she followed the line of droppings through the grass and brush. Little pieces of grass and scrub brush had been nibbled away.

The moonlight made the shadows of the trees slant and inside that oasis of darkness, she detected the faint gleam of a rabbit's fur. It was huddled in the hollow between tree roots.

As she poised, ready to throw her knife, a branch cracked somewhere close to her.

Three others were out with her and the sound should not have caught her attention but it did. She waved a hand silently for the curly-haired guard's attention, pointed in the direction of the noise, and motioned to be quiet. He passed the message to the others, all of whom froze.

The sound wasn't repeated for a few breaths, long enough for her to think she had imagined it.

Finally, a low murmur was carried on the wind along with the faint smell of smoke and heating food. Someone was camping very quietly, not in the midst of the trees but on the far side of them.

And why, she wondered, would someone go to the trouble of camping outside a stand of trees when the village was still in sight?

It seemed the others had the same questions. The group huddled together quietly and everyone crouched in the grass. No one seemed to want to speak first until Lyle held a finger up to check the wind.

Satisfied that their voices wouldn't carry to the camp, he murmured: "Well, now we're in a pickle."

Dotty looked at the trees for a moment. "Is there any chance they're merely travelers?"

Everyone shook their heads.

"Camping out here?" the man with the ginger hair asked. "Fire banked, no songs, and not in the trees? No, they're hiding from someone."

"Why d'you think they're travelers?" Lyle asked. He frowned at her.

She looked away and swallowed. Embarrassment burned in her cheeks and when she looked at the others again, she realized they were still waiting for her to speak.

"I…" It was surprisingly difficult to get the sentence out. "I heard the branch crack and I got worried," she explained. "I was concerned that something was out there that might hurt me."

Her companions simply stared at her, mystified.

It seemed she would have to spell it out. She sighed. "I'm too jumpy," she said. "I always think something's wrong and it turns out it's never a big deal. That's what Harry said, anyway." She could remember him rolling his eyes at her when she suggested they go to the hospital for a child's injury or she went downstairs to check that the door was locked at night. Still uncomfortable, she sighed again. "I'm simply used to overreacting."

The three of them shook their heads in unison.

"Ye'd better get used to *under*-reactin'," said the ginger-bearded dwarf after a moment. He shrugged. "I mean…ye see what I mean."

"He's right," Lyle said. He seemed confused but also reassured somehow. "If ye don't have yer instincts out here, ye've got nothin'. Ye have t' learn to trust yer eyes an' ears."

Dotty hunched her shoulders and nodded. "What do we do then?"

"Find out who they are," Lyle stated firmly. "Either they're here for us, or…" He frowned. "Or mayhap they're the thieves who've been stealing hay. Did anyone hear horses?"

"I did," said the older guard. "Bridles but no hooves."

"So they wrapped the hooves," Lyle mused.

"When was that reward posted?" she asked suddenly.

"Only yesterday," he said. "Why?"

The pieces came together in her head. "All the roads between here and Insea are being watched. We switched routes today, didn't we? That's what everyone was talking about and no one told me. We did that to get away from whoever was attacking the caravan. But I bet there are more mercenaries here. They know, somehow, that the others died. They've only been here a day or two, but they traveled light—and they've been stealing hay for their horses."

"Gods," Lyle whispered.

She closed her eyes as she realized something else. "And it wasn't to protect us that Per sent these two guards, was it? He did it in case I was the traitor."

He nodded wryly and the other two looked at each other in alarm.

"I didn't bother to tell you," he explained to them, "because I knew she wasn't. Trust me when I say I've seen my share of liars and thieves. No one in the caravan is either—well, except for Gwen cheating at cards every chance she gets."

"She cheats?" the older guard demanded, scandalized.

Lyle threw his hands up. "Big picture, *please.*"

"Oh. Right." He shook his head. "Sorry." Under his breath, he added, "But I'll get that ring back."

Dotty's lips twitched. "Okay, but we still need to determine who they are, right? All we have is my conjecture about them stealing hay and waiting for us. Maybe they're travelers...or refugees or something."

The second guard nodded thoughtfully.

"We should circle and cross the river," she suggested. "If they are mercenaries watching for us and we go by the road, they'll be able to see us long before we can see them."

"Plus, they'll have sentries," the curly-haired guard added. "We need to be especially careful no matter which way we go."

Lyle nodded and the group crept out of their hiding place and through the grass.

This time, they did their best to remain hidden, and they moved with exceeding stealth. She stepped around fallen branches that might crack and Lyle guided them away from the piles of leaves that would rustle. When a wolf howled somewhere nearby, everyone froze, but their targets simply continued to murmur among themselves, clearly used to the wolf's cries.

Wolf, or werewolf? Dotty shivered and looked behind her. There was nothing there but being in a world filled with unknowable magic made her superstitious. A witch could appear out of nowhere, or there might be ghosts, or—

She would not give herself nightmares. Irritated, she gave her head a stubborn shake and continued.

It was a large camp, they realized when they could finally see it. The fire was banked low and earth was piled high to keep its glow from being too visible from either the road or the village. People moved and spoke, but all of them kept their voices low. Now that the little group was closer, she could hear horses stamping sometimes, their hooves clearly wrapped.

These people were disciplined and accustomed to camping. That should be enough for her, but she didn't want to condemn people to battle and death on a "maybe."

Their group crept as close as they could.

The two guards appeared to have an entirely mimed conversation about something to do with the tents...or possibly the horses. Dotty looked on in silent bemusement and nodded when they gestured for her and Lyle to follow them to the road. Whatever they had seen, it was enough.

Dotty looked over her shoulder at the camp before she left. Metal gleamed everywhere she looked—swords, bridles, and all the tools that went with warfare. They weren't readying themselves for battle. They were like a giant cat, asleep and with its claws sheathed, but everything about them spoke of danger.

Their little group remained in the grass and didn't speak until they reached the town. The two guards looked gravely at them.

"What did you see?" Dotty asked curiously.

"Good armor," the younger said promptly. "Too good for

thieves or most mercenaries, and it's of elven make—my uncle's a blacksmith and I know their work. What they're planning to do with artifacts we're already giving the elves, though…" He shrugged.

She frowned and accepted that she could make neither head nor tail of this.

"Per might know," Lyle said, "and he needs to— If this was set up the way Dotty claims, this trap was meant to catch us one way or another, which means a large number of mercenaries and considerable money. This isn't any old ambush anymore."

"What do you mean?" she asked and stared at him in dawning horror.

"I mean," he said, "that this is probably the start of an out-and-out *war*."

CHAPTER SEVENTEEN

Although it was late when the group returned, Per was still up. He had spread maps out on the table and was in the middle of drafting several letters. When he saw Dotty, his face grew wary.

"Sir," the curly-haired guard said, "we've found something."

"And we think we solved the hay-stealing problem," Lyle added.

"That's not the point," Dotty muttered at him.

"Ye're the one who said you wanted to make a few coppers of yer own. Ye've got t' insist on payment." He patted her arm. "Ye'll learn."

She rolled her eyes. To Per, she said, "We were hunting rabbits in one of the stands of trees and we found a whole group of mercenaries. They're taking care to stay hidden from the village and they're well-equipped."

"With *elven* weapons," the guard added.

The entire tavern fell silent. Villagers and caravan members alike now paid attention. The innkeeper had stopped wiping the bar down.

Per looked at each of them in turn. "Mercenaries. Are you sure?"

They all nodded, and Lyle said flatly, "Good ones. Better than those we came across today." He gestured to her. "And Dotty has a theory as to why they're here, specifically."

"Oh, really?" He raised an eyebrow.

"You wanted to make sure I didn't know we were changing our route," she said. "You had people watch me to see if I noticed or if I knew. But these mercenaries were here even before we met the other band. *They're* the ones who have been stealing hay from the village. They're a backup force and I think we would have run into others on our original route, too. I think they're on every road between here and Insea."

Silence followed her words and Per's shoulders slumped. To her surprise, he nodded.

"I don't know the specifics," he agreed, "but whatever the case, it was set in motion before we ever left."

Everyone was quiet now, their eyes riveted on him.

"I've been suspicious from the start," he said. "The council insisted we bring more guards than we ever had before, and from what Dotty told me, those wolves should never have attacked us. The attack today...well, it was too finely coordinated for my tastes."

"What do you mean?" Dotty looked at the others, confused.

"They didn't win," Per said. "They would have in any other year but not *this* year. They only did enough damage that many of us are injured. We're battered, not broken, but if we encounter another force, we'll either break or surrender." He shook his head. "I've spread rumors in the camp since yesterday in an effort to find out who would know where we were going. I even changed the route without telling anyone and no one seemed to notice at all."

She couldn't make sense of it and shook her head in confusion, but there was no mistaking the look on his face.

"They would find us no matter which way we went," he explained. "It's a trap, and it's well-set. We've been herded through increasingly difficult tests and forced to change our route, and I have the feeling it's all been done this way to sow discord. We're supposed to turn on each other and accuse each other when we inevitably lose the caravan. The council will have someone's head on a pike by the end of this."

From the look on his face, it was clear he was referring to his own.

"Now, wait a minute," she said. "You're not simply giving up, are you?"

"There's nothing else to do," he muttered. "The farther I take this, the more lives are in danger."

"We knew what we signed up for," the older guard argued, and a few of his comrades nodded.

Per, however, shook his head. "You signed up for run-of-the-mill thieves and bandits, not a scheme that might involve the elven *army*. I don't know how many people could even pay for something like this. If I fall into their trap, they'll get the artifacts, whether you fight them or not. I might as well spare everyone."

Dotty sat heavily. Everyone looked at one another and murmured in low tones. She could hear approval, and it was clear to her that the anguish in his voice wasn't feigned. He had meant what he said when they left Berghold. He believed these artifacts were important and that the relationship between Insea and Berghold was vital to them both. Without a doubt, he believed in honoring his obligations.

He was throwing himself on his sword to save the guards.

Whoever set this up, she thought, knew he might do that. They also knew he might forge on. They'd set it up so that he would either take the blame or he'd be dead. Whatever choice he made, they didn't care about him at all.

And that made her *furious*.

"No," she said and stood. Everyone looked at her now, and she felt almost the same, dizzying sensation as when she had exhausted herself with her magic. "We won't turn back and we won't simply give up the artifacts. Whoever set this up has created layers within layers.

"They sent those other attackers to die—not elven attackers, you'll notice. They're letting *us* risk our lives, and as…he… mentioned "—she barely avoided calling the dwarf Curly-hair and instead, gestured at him—"why would the elves steal something that's going to them in the first place? Whoever this is, they're letting everyone else do their dirty work for them and I won't stand for it."

She looked around the room. The dwarves stared at her with respect but also warily.

"Do you have a plan?" Per asked her. "Because those words are all well and good, but—"

"You're not gonna like it," Dotty warned him. "But, yes. I have a plan." She sighed because she didn't like it, either. "We leave tonight. We grease the wagon wheels, wrap the horses' hooves, and take the back roads around the hay fields to stay away from where the bandits are camped. We slip past them in the night before they're looking for us, and we're gone before it's light."

After a very long silence, Per asked confusedly, "And, er…why wouldn't I like this?"

When she looked around the room, everyone was nodding, both at her plan and his question.

"Because we don't get to spend tonight in real beds," she said mournfully. "My bones may not ache as much as—well, that's not important. But a good night's rest is nothing to sneeze at, anyway."

Per laughed uproariously, the first genuinely happy sound she'd heard out of him since they'd first met—and those few days seemed like a lifetime ago. "Ah, you may be from a foreign land but you're still a dwarf," he said. "And don't worry—enough beer will put you to sleep, bed or no."

"It's my trick for sleeping under tables," Lyle told her. "It makes it much more comfortable."

Dotty prayed for patience and also made a mental note to check in on the producers of the game and make sure they were doing all right.

"We need to go now," she told Per.

He nodded and looked at the innkeeper. "Can you send anyone to guide us through the back roads?"

"Of a surety." Their host smiled. "And I think we can make some other chaos as well."

"You don't want to get mixed up with these people," she said worriedly. The thought of these villagers getting on the wrong side of an army made her feel sick to her stomach.

"Don't worry," he said confidently. "There are all kinds of things we can do to draw attention this way without making them take action. Goats getting loose, barn fires—"

"You'll set a *barn fire* simply to—"

"We'll let them handle it," Per said decisively. "Everyone, we move in no more than a quarter of an hour."

Those with a horse bolted out of their chairs like they had the devil after them, and the others began to gulp the last of their beer hurriedly.

Well, she thought, at least they had clear priorities.

It wasn't long before the wagons were assembled outside, horses raised wrapped hooves delicately, and dwarves poured grease on the cartwheels. Per moved down the line and spoke to the group around each cart in turn.

"No talking," he told them bluntly when he reached Dotty's group. "No whispering, no humming, and don't even crack your fingers. Watch where you put your feet. And if you need to do something to pass the time, for the love of all gods, pray for rain —or clouds, at least."

Everyone nodded and it wasn't long before the carts set out, moving more slowly than she would have thought possible. At this pace, however, the wheels hardly creaked.

It would have to do.

The village youngsters who were guiding them were most likely in their twenties, but to her jaded eye, they looked like they were about twelve and she fretted about involving them in this. They looked far too excited to lead the carts down a little side street and behind the fields. Nevertheless, she had to admit a small piece of her felt like she was a teenager again, sneaking out after curfew for a stolen kiss.

The kisses, the summers in the country…it had been so long since she'd thought about any of her youth. It almost made her feel younger simply to remember it.

They were twenty minutes out of town or so when the shouting began. Dotty glanced at the lights that flickered on in various windows. People ran through the streets with torches, and clatters and yells were accompanied by noisy braying.

"What happened?" she mouthed, hoping that Prima could hear her even if she didn't speak.

Thankfully, the AI could. *"They let the donkeys loose. Everyone knows not to go into the woods, so there won't be any chance of the soldiers being seen and killing them. It will merely keep their attention fixed on the town for a while.*

"Ah." She had an unexpected thought. "You know who the traitor is, don't you? If there is one."

"Mm-hmm."

"Who is it?"

"I can't tell you that."

"Won't, you mean. You won't tell me."

"Or that."

She shook her head and continued. While she knew better than to think she could persuade the AI, maybe she'd be able to outwit it at some point.

CHAPTER EIGHTEEN

The night seemed to last forever. It wasn't simply the fact that they might be set upon by soldiers at any moment. Nor was it the fact that they should be sleeping, or that they moved at a snail's pace, or that none of them could talk to one another. It was a magical combination of all of those things put together with nothing to relieve any of the fear, annoyance, or exhaustion.

They emerged from the warren of back roads several miles beyond the soldiers, at which point the tension grew so thick, Dotty was sure they could cut it with a knife. Per mandated that some of the guards begin sleeping in shifts so that they'd have a chance to be well-rested if they encountered any further patrols.

They didn't, at least not that night, and she wondered if this was because they had evaded the final step of the plan.

The sunrise was beautiful and the warmth of it very welcome. She watched the stars fade and the sky come alive with peach and gold until it deepened to a rich blue. While she understood why Per had wanted rain, she had to admit that she was pleased they hadn't gotten any.

The night had been miserable enough.

"Prima," she murmured once it became clear that they were allowed to speak once more.

"*Mmm?*"

"Did the plan work?"

The AI didn't answer.

"You won't tell me these things, even though you know and these people are in danger?"

"*These people are part of me,*" she pointed out. "*In a way, anyway.*"

"What does that even mean? Never mind. Look, I know Per is the traitor, but I can't think of a good reason." She murmured the words and paused, her heart thumping. Would the gambit work?

When Prima spoke, she could practically see the AI raising an eyebrow. "*Did you honestly think I would fall for that?*"

"Okay, new game. If I guess correctly, will you tell me?"

Prima considered this. Finally, she said, "*No.*"

"Oh, *come* on." Dotty noticed a few people look at her and gave an embarrassed smile as she tried to come up with a lie on the spot. "Uh…I'm getting a blister."

"*No, she isn't!*" Prima called. "*She's lying. She's talking to the voices in her head.*"

"Hush." It was hard to mouth the words silently when she wanted to hiss them—or spritz the AI with a water bottle like an errant cat. She decided to try a new strategy. "Come on, it must be such a clever plan. Don't you want to brag a little?"

"*Well…*" She sounded like she was considering it.

"We have so many layers to this," Dotty wheedled. "Think about it. There was the one set of bandits, then the elven army—plus wizards, if they were able to enchant wolves. How do you work all those pieces together?"

"*It was simple, if you consider—hey!*"

"Damn," Dotty muttered.

It was midday before they stopped in the shadow of the forest. Insea, Lyle had told her as they walked, was north through a little spur of the forest and around the base of a range of hills, then down onto a series of plains. The rest they enjoyed was short, only enough to water the horses and let everyone snatch a quick nap.

She had begun to reach the opinion that beer wasn't necessary for good sleep—merely exhaustion. It felt as if she had only closed her eyes when one of the guards shook her awake and the party continued.

There was an inn in the forest, Per told them, but they would stop at the far border and camp some distance from the road amongst the scree and shale. He seemed to have found a new purpose after her speech and she suspected that deep down, he was enjoying the challenge of outwitting his unknown opponents.

Dotty barely made it to the edge of the forest. The sun was definitely past its peak by then and the entire caravan was running on fumes. They moved almost as slowly as they had in order to sneak past the soldiers, and all the fun of it was gone.

She wasn't sure if anyone cooked dinner because for once, she managed to fall asleep even before she'd even thought about it.

When she woke it was almost dawn and some of the group was already moving around quietly and cooking food. There was no jerky and dried fruit on the menu today but instead, sausages and ale, as well as some kind of dark, gingery cookies that were spicy and sweet and comforting all at the same time.

Per announced that they wouldn't start for another hour to give the horses more rest and she glanced longingly at her bedroll when Lyle cleared his throat and gestured to a flat patch of ground.

"What?" she asked.

"If ye want to fight melee, ye need practice," he said. "So, up and at 'em, girl."

"Girl?"

"Are ye…" He did a double-take and looked around at the others, all of whom stared at him, equally mystified. "Are ye…" He cleared his throat and began to grow red in the face. "Are ye not a girl?" he managed finally. His voice trailed into an undignified squeak.

"I'm old enough to be your *grandmother*," Dotty said.

A second and a half later, she remembered what she looked like.

Crap.

"Ye're how old?" He no longer looked embarrassed but his jaw hung open. "Wait—how old *are* ye?"

"Eighty-four," she said with great dignity. She stood and felt her knees creak. It would seem that several days of hard walking were enough to strip all her youth away. "So show some respect."

Lyle said nothing to her, but she saw him murmur the words "eighty-four" at a guard, whose eyes were as round as dinner plates.

"All right." He bounced on the balls of his feet once they had moved away from the camp. Given the fact that they'd been on the road for several exhausting days, he was disgustingly spry and energetic. If looks could kill, she would have him dead and bagged—but since it didn't work that way, she was left only with the determination to wipe the smug grin off his face.

Unaware of this, he retrieved two small staves—the type they had used for tent poles—and tossed them to her. He placed his fist weapons aside.

"No weapons in sparring," he told her. "I'd start ye on fists but ye seem bound and determined t' run into danger an' destroy yerself, an' it's not as if we can expect to have time before our next engagement. Now, your task is simple—get in a good stab and we're done for the day."

"I thought you weren't supposed to kill with the point," she said idly. "I thought that lacked *subtlety*."

"Subtlety be damned." Lyle snorted. "It's better to be sure than subtle."

Several of the other dwarves nodded.

"Indeed." At least she could enjoy the mental image of him taking a stave to the ribs. Energetic bastard.

Dotty bounced on the balls of her feet and considered her first move. Now that no one waved real weapons around, it was difficult to get started. She still tried to find an opening when Lyle charged with a bellow.

"STOOOOOOUT!"

"Sweet Fancy Moses." She darted out of the way and gave thanks once again for her younger, more limber muscles. He careened past and she flailed with her arm but didn't land a stab, only a smack.

"Ow!" he protested.

"You're the one who wanted to—"

"STOOOOOOOOOOOUT!"

"Oh, for the love of—" She hadn't even had the chance to face him this time and simply slid forward. He barreled along behind her, unable to switch gears at a moment's notice. "Why are you being so difficult?" she snapped at him.

He merely grinned, and she realized that he enjoyed this.

And that gave her an idea. She gave a mock frown of concentration and began to try different tactics in a random series of feints to one side or another, a direct charge, or circling. It soon became a game for her in that every time he charged, she would evade him in a different way.

She didn't land very many blows over the next few minutes but she did have a good time in her efforts to become more creative. It was demanding enough that she couldn't spare either the thought or the breath for commentary.

Instead, she merely waited for her moment.

Lyle grew more and more annoyed at her silence. Now that he had no one to spar with verbally, he didn't have nearly as good a time. He managed to keep himself entertained by throwing out comments to members of the watching crowd, but Dotty could tell he wanted nothing more than to trade jabs with words as well as fists.

Well, now she knew how to get under his skin. She made a decision and, before she had the chance to think about it—and thus worry about looking stupid—unleashed a flurry of attacks. Her assault drove him across the circle far enough that the watchers scattered out of the way before she circled and began to drive him around the edge of their makeshift arena.

He didn't have the time to formulate a good counterattack, but she also didn't land any hits. She estimated that he had worked with his fists for quite some time and so was absurdly good at remaining slightly out of range of her attacks. Or slightly inside them. More than once, she slammed a stick down like a staff, only to catch the underside of her forearm on his blocking arm.

It hurt more than she expected.

Finally, with her energy running out, she did the only thing she could think of.

She threw her foot up and caught him in the ribs.

Lyle went over with an "oof" of surprise that she had to admit was deeply satisfying. He stood as Per called a five-minute warning for the caravan to leave.

"Ye didn't win," he told her, his eyes narrowed. "Ye had to stab me to win, and ye didn't land any o' those hits."

"That's as may be," Dotty said, her tone lofty. "But *you* sure didn't win, either."

A few of the watchers snickered and he gave her a smile. It was the kind of pleased smile that announced his friendship.

It also promised that the next sparring match would be much more challenging.

"Well, Dotty," she murmured under her breath, "you set yourself up for this one. You'd best get to brainstorming."

CHAPTER NINETEEN

Sweat dripped into Dotty's eyes. Her palms stung where she clutched the two wooden staves and the muscles in her back ached, desperate to give out. She told her body to dream on—she was sure as hell not giving up now. Not when she had victory in her sights.

Not a word issued from the dwarves assembled around the circle. The day's light was fading, dinner was long since over, and almost everyone had gathered to watch what had quickly become a breaktime tradition—Dotty and Lyle's sparring matches.

She circled left. Her back muscles weren't the only ones aching and her calves screamed at her.

His fists were curled loosely and he made sure to project an air of confidence, but she could see the exhaustion in him. "It's been three days," he called to her, "and ye haven't made a single good hit. Time t' give up the quest, Dotty. Go back t' bein' a wizard."

The smile she gave him looked more like a snarl than anything. "If this were a real fight, you'd have been dead ten times before breakfast."

A few people whistled at the riposte. Their match this

morning had ended with her thwacking his legs out from under him with the two staves. She still hadn't landed a blow as he'd managed to roll away and flip her sideways, but he'd have been long gone if she'd used real blades.

Wearily, she ran through what she knew. Her opponent was tired, he preferred to step back with his right leg, and he liked to duck under swings—a good thing for a dwarf if they tended to fight non-dwarves but not so useful here.

This was it. At last, this was the one and she didn't even have time to savor the moment.

Dotty rushed him, crossed in front so he could slide out of the way to his right, and pivoted. She slid low and raised her arm to flip one of the staves into a backward grip before she swept her arm sideways.

She had the immensely satisfying feeling of it jolt in her hands as it struck him point-first on the thigh. He yelled in surprise and the watching group came to their feet with a roar of approval.

Still in a long lunge, she contemplated how she would find the energy to stand but decided to fall sideways instead. It was a choice, she told herself as she tumbled. A conscious choice. She was totally in control of this situation.

STRIKING WITH THE POINT, Level 1, the screen read.

"Finally," Prima commented.

Despite the deliberately snarky tone, she didn't bother to respond. She considered both her dinner staying warm on a rock beside the firepit and her bedroll currently inside one of the tents and decided she could have a perfectly comfortable night there on the bare ground. No amount of comfort was worth the effort of standing right now.

Which made it all the more annoying when a boot nudged her in the ribs and flipped her onto her back. Lyle's face swam into view.

"Urgh," she said in protest.

"Tired, are ye?"

"No. You're merely so ugly."

The dwarves laughed and clapped, and her opponent grinned. Dwarves had reached the point where they took pride in everything the other races disliked about them—short, big-footed, and with bulbous noses and a distinct trend toward hairiness.

He offered her a hand and held it out until she clasped it reluctantly and let him pull her to her feet. She gazed longingly at her dinner happily when he spoke.

"Again."

"Wait, *what?*" Dotty looked at him so sharply her neck muscles snapped. She rubbed the side of her neck with a wince. "*What?*" she repeated.

Lyle threw the two staves at her and smiled when she moved to catch them without thinking. "I said, do it again."

"But we've been sparring for…" She didn't have a watch. "And I landed a hit. And…*food.*"

"Battles don' wait," he said philosophically. "Again, *Zauberer.*"

The rest of the group clapped. First, they had been overawed to have her in the group and then, they had mistrusted her. But since her innocence had been proven and they had seen her in action, they had warmed to her considerably.

There weren't many dwarven wizards, although their earth magic was some of the strongest in the world. Dwarves preferred to make something physical—a sculpture, a piece of jewelry, or a building. In the same way, they preferred to change their world through direct action rather than through magic.

Consequently, they deeply approved of her wanting to learn melee combat when she was already a wizard.

Dotty sighed and looked at the sticks in her hands. She had to admit, a certain part of her was interested to see if she could reproduce her results. It had been a long few days while she successfully attempted maneuver after maneuver and learned different ways to step and dodge.

But she hadn't landed a strike with the point until now, and she wanted to see if this had been a fluke or not.

"All right, Stout." She banished the tiredness in her muscles and straightened. "One more match and the winner gets the other's beer for dinner."

The cheer this time was deafening, and he nodded at her with a grin.

"You have yourself a deal."

DuBois snatched another bag of popcorn off the desk and opened it without looking at it. He didn't know which flavor it would be, which was the best way to snack it—there were only *good* unknowns, as far as he was concerned.

The first crunch was heavenly and rich. Good old caramel corn, he thought. It was perfection, everything popcorn should be—sweet, comforting, and crunchy.

He smiled as he watched the data stream from Dotty's game. The others liked to watch it on a monitor which provided a third-person view of the scene, but he had always preferred the raw data.

There was so much more there, for one thing. Simply by increasing her heart rate regularly over the past weeks, her cardiovascular fitness had gone up considerably. Certain muscles, triggered subconsciously by her mind, began to show signs of strength without the usual wear and tear. Her sleep cycles had become more regular and easier to slip into, which meant she was more alert during her waking periods.

And her brain, long-since trained to view muscle fatigue or joint pain as something frightening, slowly learned to revel in physical exhaustion. She showed increased resiliency to everything—and that meant she was able to take joy in far more experiences than she would have before.

The three PIVOT members—who the doctor had come to regard affectionately as nephews and a niece, having had experience only with his siblings' children—had joined him while he watched. Jacob was eating a burrito of some kind, and the others sipped coffee.

"Is she still fighting?" Nick asked. "She was fighting when we left. How much time has passed in-game?"

"They're starting another round," DuBois said. "It's incredible. The more she learns, the easier the learning gets. Her brain is showing increased plasticity. I'll run that against Justin's data soon." He held a hand up. "Wait, match two is starting."

Everyone clustered around to watch.

Dotty held her mock blades slanted across her body, both raised. This was one of the earliest and most humiliating lessons she had learned. A blade at her side was no use if her opponent could close the distance between them quickly, and Lyle was *damned* quick.

It was also embarrassing that it had taken her so long to beat him when she had ranged weapons and he didn't. On the other hand, she told herself that he'd spent his entire life training and she had only recently learned to fight with daggers and short swords during their sparring.

Level Thirty-seven in Stamina and Level Eighteen in Fake Short Swords wasn't so bad when she looked at it from that perspective.

Lyle charged with a shout, but she had learned how to respond to that. As he drew breath, she braced herself for the sound and watched his core. The way he moved there would show her where to move out of the way. He was coming in to her left, the way she usually circled, and she increased speed to evade him.

She turned as she slid out of the way. Her staves were at the ready and he didn't have a good path in, not without losing this match almost immediately.

He didn't wait even a moment before he attacked again. He was quick on his feet and tireless—she'd heard about feats of combat ranging from werewolves to wizards, not to mention a giant tournament in Insea. She wasn't sure how many of these stories she believed but she had begun to see how even someone who didn't fight with weapons could have had such a long career.

His onslaught didn't leave her much time to react, but she'd learned that she didn't need it. She swung both staves in a circular pattern and interlocked them so there was neither a break in her guard nor a particular area for him to pivot to next. He was forced to cut his charge short and she immediately began her retaliatory attack.

Dotty drove him back across the circle and suddenly realized that she didn't feel the pain in her muscles in quite the same way anymore. While she was certainly tired, both the raw feeling in her throat and the burn in her thighs had transformed almost completely into a feeling of pure joy.

Clarity dawned with a kind of raw pleasure. She *loved* this.

She didn't have to think through the actions anymore and simply thought of where she wanted to be and her body obeyed. She had one startled moment of memory that her body wasn't doing *any* of this but banished the thought. After all those years spent arguing that books and games weren't real, she had found that she no longer cared about the distinction.

This was real—this moment, with the sweat on her skin, the breeze in her hair, and with her target ahead of her.

Her one moment of distraction had been enough for Lyle, though. He lunged, threw his arms up and out in an arc to bat her blades away, and dropped his shoulder to drive it into her stomach. She was carried up and had one sickening moment to realize what was coming before she landed hard on her back.

The fall didn't quite manage to knock the wind out of her. She shoved him away and rolled before the pain could surge, something she had learned was essential, and began an attack before she fully recovered. Experience had taught her that as soon as she stopped moving, she opened herself up to an attack.

A battle was no time for recuperation.

Dotty saw the opening only a few moments later. He would follow the weapons, not her body. He had fixed on that as the thing to avoid.

It wasn't a terrible idea, but it left him open.

She began another attack. Her makeshift blades spun and wove and Lyle evaded them with practiced ease. But as she whirled, both blades went left and he predictably slid away, and she planted both her feet and drove her hips back to collide with his.

From the *oof* sound he made in her ear, she had struck something important. Unsure if it was his sternum or something rather more fragile, she said a silent prayer for his forgiveness, ducked slightly, and stood and tipped her torso forward to flip him over her shoulder.

He landed like a ragdoll with his arms open, and she was able to kneel and drive one staff down. She stopped at the last moment to the sound of an appreciative gasp from the crowd.

Then, mindful of the rules, she let the stave poke his stomach.

Lyle struggled to take a breath—it seemed she'd struck his sternum instead of something that would require more profuse apologies—but he grinned broadly. He propped himself up on his elbows a few moments later and nodded at her.

"I said to do it again, and ye did it again. Well fought. My ale is yours."

"Nah." Dotty hauled him up. "I have first watch, remember? Anyway, you need to keep your strength up. We have much more sparring to do."

She settled down to eat with congratulations and shoulder

claps from the dwarves nearby. From the chatter around her, the latest set of rear scouts had returned and there was still no sign of pursuit. The rest of the caravan seemed pleased and toasts were made to Per's ingenuity.

But when she looked up from a mouthful of food, she caught the caravan leader staring back along the road. His face showed the same troubled feeling she had fought for days now.

No one as well-equipped and well-moneyed as their traitor would simply give up now.

There was a fight coming. It was only a matter of when.

CHAPTER TWENTY

Yunien J'Alar, newly appointed to his command in the elven army, began to think that he was being duped. He read the letter once again before he rolled it into its leather case and stared at it.

The tent flap parted and Guril, his most trusted friend, entered with a smile and a plate of food. He put it in front of the commander, took the leather cylinder with a question in his eyes, and—at his friend's nod—drew the letter out and read it.

Guril sank onto one of the camp stools while the other elf ate. Rations tonight were the same as they had been for days—dried meat, dry road-bread, and strips of fruit, with a sprig of dried herbs to keep the breath fresh.

There was no call to be entirely unmannerly, after all, even when they were so far away from proper food and lodging.

"You don't think much of this, it seems," he said when Yunien looked up.

"We've spent days following these leads." The commander shook his head. "If they're lying about what road they're on, it'll be bad for us."

He had pushed his soldiers at a breakneck pace over the past few days since he'd realized that the dwarven caravan had slipped away from him. Whether it was a lucky chance that they'd taken the back roads, he didn't know. Exactly like he didn't know whether they had orchestrated the donkeys getting loose in one dwarven village or whether they had simply taken advantage of the opportunity.

All he knew was that the caravan full of artifacts had arrived and in the morning, it had been gone without a trace.

Yunien did not intend to let them escape again. He was loyal to the elven monarchy above all else. Where Insea had once been the shining example of his people's prowess, it had long since faded into obscurity, welcomed humans and dwarves into its nobility, allowed orcish traders, and ceased to issue even the most mild statements regarding the elves.

No one had seen the king in years and even before that, he had not responded when a minor member of the royal line established a new monarchy in the forests of Juranil.

The elves had once ruled this world and they would do so again. He was devoted to that ideal. While he had never seen Berghold, he had seen drawings and considered it a dank cave. The human towns were nothing to brag about either, and their cities were squalid hellholes. The orcs, meanwhile, still traveled like nomads across the eastern plains.

And Ynsi'i, the jewel of the elves, was now known as Insea—a bastardization, the closest their script or their clumsy tongues could come to imitating the true name.

Yunien did not know all of his king's plan to restore power to the elves. He knew there would be a new city, more beautiful than Insea by far, and there would be envoys and armies marching. The plan would take many generations, even by the long-lived standards of the elves.

He prided himself on not needing to know the full magnitude of it. All he knew was his portion—to find this shipment of artifacts steeped in the earth magic of the dwarves and the stolen magic of the elves and bring them to the elves' temporary home in Tormari. For years, these priceless artifacts had been sent to Insea to serve a king who would not put his people first and also the rabble that now filled those streets. His king had sent many envoys over the years to remind the dwarves of their loyalty to the elves and ask them to redirect their shipments.

They had not and in doing so, had defied their rightful ruler.

The king had placed his trust in Yunien when he asked the young commander to right this one wrong, and he would not fail. He had contacted sources deep within Berghold and spent long months bartering through an untraceable set of contacts until he finally found a source willing to give everything away for gold.

Gold—what a small thing compared to a love of one's people. Such traitorous behavior only showed why the dwarves should not rule anything at all.

Their source had promised that the caravan would arrive, battered and close to defeat, at a certain elven village. For all Yunien knew, that had happened.

And then everything had gone wrong.

"D'you trust our source?" Guril asked curiously.

Yunien straightened. "Speak properly," he commanded. "And of course I do not trust our source. It is a traitor—a *dwarven* traitor. But our readings showed that we were close to the artifacts at the village. We know their destination and can only hope we will intercept them once more. And then the traitor...will be found."

Guril raised an eyebrow curiously. "What will happen to them?" There had been extensive debate around the campfires about what should be done with this dwarf. After all, they had turned on their king. On the other hand, they had turned on their king to support the primacy of the elves. Should they be punished or rewarded?

Only another inferior species could make such a muddle of

things, Yunien thought contemptuously. He did not envy the king that decision.

"I did not ask," he said and congratulated himself once again on his unwavering, unquestioning loyalty. "We will find their traitor and bring them to the king. What he does will doubtless be just and wise. Tell the camp to pack up. We will travel through the night."

Guril did not protest, knowing better than to voice displeasure with the orders. The soldiers would be disappointed to not have any sleep, but they were the finest, hardiest warriors in the elven army—they would march on, long past the endurance of others.

And the artifacts would be in elven hands once more.

The elves were fools.

Only fools, after all, became so estranged from their king that they formed another monarchy without war and began to send imperious directives to the other races based on nothing at all.

The traitor agreed, wholeheartedly, that Insea should not have the dwarven artifacts that were sent each year. The debt had long since been paid and what had Insea done for Berghold? Nothing within living memory. It was a city ruled by a king who didn't even care to show his face, and the elves had put up with that for far too long.

They liked to think of themselves as great warriors too. The traitor gave a little laugh at that idea. Any real warrior would have conquered Insea or come in force to demand Berghold's loyalty but they had not.

Clearly, they *could* not.

The artifacts that would be stolen this year were a small price to pay for the war that would break out now. The new elven king, still gathering his strength, would earn the ire of the dwarves as well as the retribution of the ruler of Insea. The humans would know the elves for the traitors they were, and the orcs were essentially irrelevant.

In fact, they didn't seem to care about anything beyond their hunts and their rituals. They could be a mighty force if they ever had a mind to be. It was as well that they didn't.

The elves might fall first in name but it would be the humans who fell first in truth. They would be seduced by the gold in the dwarven vaults and the weakness of their scattered leaders. Without a drop of blood being spilled, they would join with the dwarves, accept gifts and envoys, and would become dwarven citizens.

Their joint victory over the elves would be the last the humans knew of themselves as a sovereign species. They could do what they did best—trade, make coin, and farm. The dwarves wouldn't interfere with that. Perhaps some kings could live on as puppets of the dwarven monarchy. The dwarves would recoup all they had spent and more.

The battle would wipe out the fledgling new elven monarchy before it had even truly begun. It would show the elves their true place in the world and finally—*finally*—the dwarves would begin to establish the dominance they deserved.

They wouldn't rule from Berghold. It was only one city. Dwarves had existed before the elves came. They'd had their magic and their traditions and would make future cities, grander and more powerful. Their wizards would rule over all others.

The traitor adjusted his cloak and looked around at the landscape. He was so close to this, the thing he had worked toward for years. For decades, he had accompanied the caravans, overseen the stonemasons, and watched as the limitless talents of the dwarves were usurped and bled away.

The elven commander—for he was not as stealthy as he

thought, that one—had been a stroke of well-timed luck. He was so eager to play his part. So ready to fall upon the caravan and slaughter the guards.

The traitor smiled.

Soon. It would all come together very soon.

CHAPTER TWENTY-ONE

Dotty awoke to a strange thrumming sound at her wrist, opened her eyes, and realized groggily that the tent was flooded with blue light. She sat up in alarm and glanced at the bracelet, which glowed.

Justin had told her it would let her contact her family. Curious, she flipped it. Somehow, the light had not woken the other two women with whom she shared the tent and neither of them even stirred when she took the amulet off her wrist and the glow intensified.

Was she the only one who could see it?

Most likely. She brushed her fingers over the glowing blue surface and was surprised when the world around her froze. In front of her was a picture of parchment and words appeared as if written out by hand.

Dotty—

This is Justin. You've taken to the game very well and you're learning weapons quickly. Keep the book, though. I think you may want to try magic again someday. You're a natural at that too. It would be a shame if you didn't try.

She snorted. Sure, she might read some of the book every

night and imagine new, innovative ways to use her powers, but she didn't intend to *use* them.

Without a doubt, she wouldn't.

Definitely not.

To reinforce her resolve, she shook her head.

Your family wanted to throw a party for you for your birthday, the letter continued. *We asked if they would be willing to come to the lab. As you have been inside the pod for some time, we do not want to run the risk of exhausting you. However, bringing you out of the pod would also give us useful data before you return to the game (if you wish to do so).*

Let us know if you would like us to plan this party for you. Your daughter-in-law has assured me she will make your favorite chocolate espresso cake and will make sure someone brings brandy instead of telling you it's not good for your health.

Dotty snickered. That would be Mary. As a doctor, John liked to remind his mother about which things were healthy and which were not. His list of vices inevitably included almost everything that made life worth living.

His wife, on the other hand, loved to bake—and cheerfully, irreverently kept John in line while she was at it. She had been a good match for him from the start.

Dotty realized now that she missed her family. She read on, biting her lip.

If there is anything you need in the game, let us know. We promise you will have a good chance to use your skills soon. Stay on your guard.

-Justin

P.S. To respond, press down on the blue button and it will record your voice.

With the world frozen behind the letter, she took some time to simply think. She curled her knees to her chest and rested her chin on them, something she would not have imagined doing weeks before. The residual soreness of sleeping on the ground was already working its way out of her muscles, and she felt invigorated and ready to start her day.

But she wanted to think before she accepted any offers to leave. It had been hard enough to go through with this once, and what would she feel like if she went back? Would her body be a prison? Would her children cry and talk her out of returning?

Would she, for some reason, not *want* to return?

Oddly enough, that thought scared her more than the others. She was someone here—not someone famous or all-powerful but someone who had a place and a mission. No matter what else she might encounter, she couldn't leave these people undefended.

She pressed the blue button and began to speak.

"Justin, thank you for your kind words about my skills, although I confess it made me much more self-conscious to remember that everyone in the lab has seen my failures.

"I am enjoying the game immensely and have signed on as a guard for a dwarven caravan." She assumed he knew, given that he could see her progress and also because he had set the whole thing up to start with. "I can't leave the game until the shipment is safely delivered to Insea, which will be in about five days— although if it's close to my birthday, it must have been longer outside the game than inside it.

"I would like to see everyone, however, so I will be ready to come out of the game any time after that. Thank you very much. Dotty."

She released the button and stared around the tent before she said quietly, "Prima, you can start the game again."

The AI didn't do so immediately. "*I am not good with human emotions when I do not create them myself. Are you angry or are you upset?*"

Dotty grimaced. "I'm frightened," she said honestly. "I'm a different person here than I am in the real world. Giving that person up was difficult and now, giving this person up is difficult too. I'm afraid I won't ever be able to come back to her."

Prima considered this. *"Are you not both people?"*

"People change over time. If my family tells me something that steals the joy from the game…" She shrugged.

"You seem like quite a stubborn person. I can't see them managing to change your opinion without a very good set of reasons."

She smiled. "Have I ever mentioned that I appreciate you?"

"No," Prima said promptly. Then, she asked curiously, *"Why did you change the subject?"*

"It wasn't a subject change." She grinned and threw the covers back. "See if you can figure out that one. If you want to keep time frozen, I can cook breakfast for everyone before they wake."

"And have them burn you as a witch? I don't think you want that." Prima unfroze time and the snores of her tentmates resumed.

Dotty smiled and headed outside to where Per was seated by the embers of the previous night's fire, smoking a pipe in deep contemplation. He looked at her in surprise.

"Couldn't you sleep?"

She shrugged. Aside from the fact that she didn't feel like coming up with any particular lie, she'd learned over the years that if you didn't say anything, other people merely filled in your answer in their heads. Instead, she sat across the fire from him and looked at the eastern horizon. "What about you?"

Per hesitated. "Nightmares," he said finally. "I've been with the caravan almost every year since I was young. I started as a guard, then an envoy, and I've escorted everyone from princesses to goldsmiths. We've passed through battlegrounds and I worried sometimes about the caravan, but…never like this."

Dotty frowned. "What was your nightmare?"

"I was lost in a forest," he said, glanced over his shoulder to where the last trees had finally faded away, and shuddered. "I don't like forests. If you have a roof over your head, it should be stone, not something living with a mind of its own. That's the elves for ye, though. Anything simple, they can turn into a piece of their magic."

She smiled at that. Many of the dwarves reveled in their brogue, an almost-Scottish accent that reminded her of an old school friend. A few like Per, however, only slipped into it when they were lost in thought or especially upset about something.

"So, you were in a forest…" she prompted.

"There was someone following me," he continued. "Or…us? I'm not sure if it was only me or if the whole caravan was there. I could hear my breathing. I struggled to get away and I thought I had done it, but then I felt something behind me, and…" His shoulders had hunched and he looked embarrassed. "It's not important. They say dreams are nothin' but our fears, the ones we won't let ourselves see in the light o' day. I don't think this is too mysterious, though. And I've been worried about it during the days as well as the nights."

"Yeah." Dotty stared at the sunrise. "I always thought that advice was crap, too."

Per snorted, spat, and checked to see if his pipe was still lit. "No nightmares for you, then?"

"None these days." She managed a smile. "It's been a long time since…well, since I've remembered my dreams."

"Yes, I recall you saying you're eighty-four." He smirked. "What's more impressive, to be honest, is that you managed to convince the rest of them of it."

"I haven't always been in *this* body," she said.

The alarm on his face let her know she'd spoken incorrectly. "Let me state, for the record, that I have not taken this body from anyone. I mean—look, this has only ever been *my* body. There's no demonic possession going on or anything. I merely had a different life…once."

He put his pipe down and looked at her. "Were you always a dwarf?"

"No," she admitted. "Once, I was a human. I had a husband, children, grandchildren…great-grandchildren." She looked away.

"What happened?"

"Nothing. Years and years of nothing, and dreams fading, and my world getting smaller and smaller." Dotty remembered the story she'd heard from Justin and Lyle. "And then a young man from my world, a man named Justin, came from this place, and told us that warriors were needed."

"Justin…the man who won the tournament at Insea?" Per looked dumbfounded.

"Yes. He…put the call out in our world and I answered. My family is safe but it seems yours—your world—may not be."

Per looked at her with new respect. "So that's who you truly are. Not a dwarf, not one of us at all, but a spirit carried between worlds and given a new form. Imagine where else you might have ended up." He snorted. "You could have been an orc."

"I chose where I would land," Dotty said. "I chose the dwarves. I wanted to know more about them. I saw a picture of…well, me." She gestured to her body. "She looked like a woman who cared more about mining jewels than wearing them. She looked like a person I had never allowed myself to be."

"Can I ask you something?" Per asked.

"Of course."

"If that's why you're here—to be a hero, to step out of a small life and save us all—to become *more*—why are you so afraid of your magic?"

She looked sharply at him.

He shrugged. "But, what do I know, eh? I'm only fifty. A spring chicken."

"You're right about that. My youngest child is older than you." She shook her head. "And what good will I do anyone if I die?"

"Will your…would you be able to go back?"

"I don't know."

Per looked at her with a new appreciation now. "You didn't know us but you came to help us."

"Do you believe me?" Dotty asked.

"I wouldn't, but I heard the stories from Insea weeks back—

and heard, too, that there was a certain dwarf who fought with Justin in the tournaments. He told me Justin's story before I heard it from you, and he told me he had vouched for you. I think…well, I always assumed that he simply meant somewhere far beyond the sea, not another world entirely." He shook his head. "Either way, I've seen many liars in my day—well, politicians, anyway—and you don't strike me that way. You're too no-nonsense. I have a feeling that if you decided you wanted to hijack the caravan, you'd come up to me and ask straight out what it would take."

She was surprised into a laugh. "You're not far off. Honestly, though, it seems like too much trouble. Besides, you clearly cared about what you said when we were leaving Berghold, and trust me, alliances that are strong should be kept that way. That means honoring commitments."

"Well said." Per stood and stretched. "Shall we make breakfast for the rest of them? It's five days to Insea if we travel fast and I, for one, don't want to spend a minute longer than I have to waiting for whatever ambush is in store down the road."

"So both o' ye think we're headed into a trap too?" Lyle had emerged from his tent and he wandered over to start stoking the fire. "I have the same feeling. I'm merely hoping that whoever we meet next, it's not orcs."

"*Orcs?*" the other two said at the same time.

He waved his hands. "It was supposed to be a joke."

"That is a terrible joke," Per said.

"What he said." Dotty pointed.

"Oh, lighten up—although I now know how t' get everyone's attention, eh? I only meant, we've been attacked by humans and elves so far, right? So orcs would be next."

Dotty could see his reasoning now but she still shook her head. "Bad joke. Still a bad joke."

"Yeah, yeah, so ye've said. Tell ye what, the two o' ye can split my ale ration for the day."

"Done," they said together. She thought they were getting rather good at that.

"Oh, come on. Ye're not going to take me up on that?"

"Of course I am," she told him flatly. "Just feel lucky we're not making you carry us."

CHAPTER TWENTY-TWO

The day dawned clear and bright but clouds began to move in by midmorning. Dotty, at first, registered this only as a welcome relief from the blazing sun, but it wasn't long before the first spatter of rain landed on her head.

She looked up and swore. The cloud that was raining on them was airy and wispy and blue sky showed around the edges. Moving in behind it were clouds of progressively darker gray and lightning crackled in the distance.

There wasn't anything to do except keep moving. The rain went from an occasional spatter to a full drizzle, enough to soak everything. She wrapped her cloak tightly around her as she walked. Rain wasn't so bad when you had a warm, dry house to go to—not to mention a change of clothes—but when you knew you'd have wet socks for the rest of the day...well, *then* rain was miserable.

The road began to wind into a gorge and she looked at the slick and shiny walls. Perhaps this had been a quarry once, she thought, although the road was narrow.

Could someone have gone to all the trouble of cutting a single road through the rock? And, if so, to what purpose?

"All the roads to Insea are like this," a voice said briskly.

Dotty looked up as Lyle stepped beside her.

He smiled and rain ran in rivulets down his beard. "The roads to Insea are narrow. Some have drop-offs on both sides and some are like this. They should get flooded or crumble, but they don't. It must be one of their spells. You can always get there but the thing is, you can't get an *army* there very easily."

She nodded.

"It's been nigh on a millennium since Insea was built," he said, speaking loudly over the sound of the rain. "It's never seen war, even since the king disappeared. No one visibly rules it and there's no official army, only royal guards, but it's always been at peace, even though it's so prosperous."

"Prosperity breeds peace," she pointed out.

"Within a country, aye." He raised an eyebrow. "But it also breeds envy."

Dotty nodded. She opened her mouth to speak when something clattered against the stone wall nearby. With a glance at one another, she and Lyle went to check.

"Why are we looking?" she asked a moment later. She had cut her hand on a particularly sharp rock and proceeded to drop it on her other hand and into a puddle. The resulting splash flicked mud onto her face. She sat on her haunches and looked at Lyle.

"If it's a rock," Lyle said, still studying the area, "mayhap we all get out of the gorge."

"Oh. But there are tons of rocks, how will we know—"

"Aha!" He pulled something out of the rocks. "It was an arrow." He smiled at her.

She looked meaningfully at him.

"Oh, shit," he said.

Somewhere ahead, lost in the rain, the shout went up. "Attack! *Attack!*"

They leapt to their feet and looked around. There was no way to see the high edges of the canyon, but clatters sounded all around them.

"Take yer cloak off!" Lyle yelled to her. "They can't see much in this rain, but they can sure as hell see *ye!*"

It was a good thought. She yanked at the laces that held her cloak in place and threw it into the back of a cart. Both of her daggers were already in her hands before she realized how useless they were. What would daggers do against arrows?

"I think you know what to do," Prima said.

"Oh, you have to be kidding me," Dotty snapped. "Did you set this up?" Another arrow clattered and she threw herself sideways.

"Not with this particular goal in mind."

"When this is over, we will have a *talk.*" She picked herself up and hissed at the pain of her bruises as she clambered into the back of a cart. "Lyle! Can we turn the carts? I can cover our retreat if so—and take care of those archers!"

He scrambled in beside her. "What did ye say? How will ye cover a retreat wi' two daggers, lass?"

"Magic!" Dotty bellowed over the rain. "And unless you have any *better* ideas—"

But Lyle was already gone and he darted through the rain to the front of the caravan.

She sighed and wished he *had* had a better idea.

There was nothing for it, though. She crouched among the bales of cloth and supplies and tried to still her mind. The cart jostled as the horse shied and reared, and the arrows continued to hiss and clatter against the rock walls. They didn't hit much, but no individual arrow needed to.

Their enemy knew they were pinned.

Frantically, she sifted through the spells in her head. Stone-Shock? What could she do with that?

An idea came to her in the next moment. She peeked over the edge of the cart and, as the wind gusted, she thought she saw the line of archers at the top of the gorge. Each stood tall, drew a bowstring back, and aimed at the caravan.

Cowards.

Dotty tried her idea with one of them and fixed her focus on the bow. What she pictured in her head was the rock dropping on her hand and splashing into the puddle only this time, the rock was somehow wrapped around the bow.

A few points of her magic left her in a whoosh, and somewhere above, she heard a yelp. A few moments later, a bow tumbled down the slope—unfortunately, not still clutched by its owner.

Well, one couldn't have everything. She squinted enough to see the rock around the edge of it and smiled. There was nothing like taking your aim carefully and having the weight of your weapon suddenly shift on you.

She looked at her magic bar and shook her head. There wasn't nearly enough to eliminate all of them.

She could throw them off, though. At random, she chose her targets and added lumps of rock to some bows or hurled rocks at others. It didn't eliminate their enemies and only put their ranks in disarray, but that would have to be enough for now.

Far too slowly, the carts began to turn and Dotty cursed inwardly as she tried to maintain her focus. She had gotten used to the speed of modern life with cars that could turn quickly and accelerate out of a confrontation. Not that she had ever been in a comparable situation, of course, but her closest comparison to this ambush was a movie car chase.

In this case, there was nowhere to run easily.

How had she not seen this coming?

"Dotty!" Lyle jumped beside her. "Whatever yer doin', the archers have stopped firing. Come on!"

She followed him without a thought. Her magic was almost exhausted, and she could still hear the shouts of alarm behind her. The two of them dodged between carts being pulled by panicked horses and it wasn't long before she realized that she could hear the clash of weapons.

Of course there had been a ground force.

"How many?" she called to her companion.

His answer was one grim word. "Enough."

Dotty increased her pace. If she slowed, she would turn and run. She didn't want to do this again—she didn't want to fight and kill—but there wasn't any other option.

"I hate this," she muttered to Prima.

"You wanted to bring good to this world."

"This isn't *real!*" she snapped as she reached the front of the battle line and whirled into action. She cut down an elf without even thinking about it, whirled, and slashed down his—or possibly her—front. The elf staggered back with a scream and she shifted her dagger to a back grip before she stabbed sideways into another elf's ribs.

Prima's answer almost made her stop dead. *"It is to me,"* she said.

And if she didn't help her fix it, the AI would be stuck with these bastards winning the battle.

The first enemy she'd slashed at was on their feet again and snarled as they drew a sword. Dotty threw her foot up to punch at the elf's knee and brought the pommel of one dagger down on their head when they fell, clutching their leg.

"Dotty!" Per's call was panicked.

She turned to see a tall and strapping elf with blond hair pulled back in a severe braid. From the excessive shine of the armor and the golden torc at their neck, she guessed this was a champion or commander of some kind.

For the first time, she was *very* aware of how short she was in this body. Dotty backed away slowly and adjusted her hands on the grips of her daggers.

A movement flickered at the corner of her eye and she noticed Lyle trying to sneak around the side of the battle.

Which made her play quite clear. She sneered at the elf and spread her arms in a mocking gesture. "So you thought you'd shoot us like fish in a barrel, huh? No honor among thieves, I guess."

The elf narrowed his eyes. "We are not thieves." The voice was unmistakably male.

Well, that was one mystery solved.

"Okay." She made a mocking finger quote gesture. "Fancy canyon pirates."

He raised his sword. "These goods are ours. We have sent word to the dwarves informing them of this. They have refused to see reason. The elves are now forced to shed blood to take possession of what is ours by right."

"STOOOOOOUT!" bellowed a familiar voice.

The warrior whirled—for all his ridiculous posing and cowardice, he seemed to be quite well trained—and she darted in to jab a dagger at the gap between the panels of his arm guards. She darted out of the way again as he was bowled past her by the force of Lyle's tackle.

Dotty had been so focused on surviving that she hadn't thought beyond each swipe and slash, but for the first time, she allowed herself to imagine victory.

She might have been slightly premature on that because the very fancy elf had barely landed when one of the others yelled, "The commander!"

There were no more than a dozen of them, but at the threat to their leader, they formed into a tight knot and rushed in from all sides. She grasped Lyle's hand and hauled him clear, and the dwarves began to back away. The carts grew more distant with each moment.

"Only a few minutes," she called to the rest, all bloodstained and pale and heaving for breath. "We only have to give them time to get away."

The elven commander laughed at that. One of his soldiers had helped him up and he stared at the dwarves with contempt and a trace of both mockery and pity.

And she knew, in an instant, that they had planned for this far better than she had even guessed.

That was enough of a surprise to her, but the far greater surprise was that she wasn't frightened. She was *furious*. The rage melted through her in a wash of heat and she raised her dagger and threw before she had a chance to think.

It burrowed into the elven commander's eye, and he collapsed in a heap.

After a moment of complete silence, both sides of the group charged. Dotty streaked through the line of charging elves to reclaim her dagger—that was the problem with throwing blades, she thought to herself—and turned to try to catch the back of an elf's leg. He fell screaming, and she leapt into the fray.

The elf who had helped the commander to his feet lunged at her, his eyes crazed. "Dwarven scum!"

She feinted right and dove left, rolled awkwardly, and winced before she bounced to her feet. Her muscles were sore and she was tired, but this was how she had learned to fight. While he still tried to stop and turn, she had already initiated her attack.

It happened so quickly it surprised her. She no longer planned her combat move by move and simply pushed into motion. Her momentum helped her into a slide with her left hand out to brace herself, and she barely felt the impact when she landed. Her feet struck the elf's ankles and he began to topple. His hands lurched out instinctively in search of a way to regain his feet.

He thudded onto the point of one of her daggers. His face slammed into the rock next to hers and his dead weight sprawled on her.

Panic surged through her but a moment later, his body was hauled away and Per offered her a hand.

"Come on!" he called, as he hauled her up. Dead elves lay around them and she identified two dwarves among the corpses.

Per's face was white with either blood loss or fury, perhaps both. "We have to get to the front of the caravan," he yelled to them. "Burials later. Protect the rest *now!*"

That was what they needed to turn them from where they stared brokenly at the bodies of their friends and they raced away toward the caravan. Dotty ran with them, all her attention focused on the coming battle. She had fallen, been bruised and scraped, and probably sprained one of her hands, but none of that mattered. They had defeated this group of elves and they could deal with the rest.

At the top of the hill, however, they skidded to a halt. Facing them was easily an entire company of soldiers, waiting in ranks in front of the stopped caravan.

One rider trotted forward and his gaze scanned the group.

"Where," he asked crisply, "is Commander j'Alar?"

Lyle sighed beside her and she glanced at him, but he shook his head.

"End of the road," the dwarf murmured sadly. "I didn't think I'd go out like this."

Dotty looked from him to the elves. There had to be some way to save them. If she confessed…well, she didn't know if she would die in the real world, but she couldn't leave them all here, could she?

She was about to step forward when a horn rang clear and dramatically in the silence.

The elves turned and their ranks rippled, and the dwarves uttered a whoop.

"What? What is it?" She looked around in confusion.

"It's a dwarven battle horn." Lyle laughed and the color had returned to his cheeks. "It looks like we have a chance after all. Come on, ye bloody bastards. Let's make some stories for the songs!"

CHAPTER TWENTY-THREE

The battle was in disarray almost from the beginning. The cavalry, which had been ready to charge, swept to the flanks to reach the rear attacking force and left the foot soldiers to scramble without orders. The chaos was exacerbated when two of their sergeants issued different commands.

They still called questions to each other when the entire horde of dwarven guards descended on them. In short order, it became clear that these elves did not care nearly so much about the caravan as their commander had.

"Mercy!" one of them yelled.

"We surrender!" called another.

"Fight on, you fools!" The sergeant was almost purple in the face as he fought Per, who ducked and backpedaled to avoid his wild swings. "So they're armed. You are too!"

"The cavalry are dead!" One of the soldiers gestured pleadingly at the back of the line. Screams and shouts still issued from that direction, but Dotty saw very few blond riders still atop horses.

"Aye." Per grunted. "Ye didn't prepare for a well-armed force, did ye? Instead, ye thought ye could slaughter us an' walk away with the artifacts." He stumbled as he avoided another swing, and she could see he was tiring. His age counted against him and he'd been injured with barely a few days to recuperate while he slept under the stars and ate travel rations.

He was still a dwarf and exceedingly canny, however. When he lured the elven sergeant into a deep lunge, he kicked his supporting leg out and lopped his head off with one heavy stroke.

Appalled, she clapped a hand over her mouth and only narrowly missed losing her head when her opponent swiped wildly, as horrified as she was.

Dotty seized the moment to stab him in the stomach as she wasn't quite tall enough to aim comfortably for the chest. It rubbed her the wrong way somewhat to fight on after an opponent had argued for surrender but on the other hand, Per was right. These elves had come to slaughter the caravan and leave with the treasure.

She was on the last of her reserves of energy when the dwarven cavalry broke through the last of the elven ranks. They pulled up sharply when they saw the dwarven soldiers and a moment later, one of the riders urged his horse forward at a trot. He swung down from his horse, removed his helmet, and clasped Per's hand.

"*Councilor?*" the caravan leader asked, dumbstruck.

"We received word of the attack three days after you left," Marwitz explained. His chest heaved and his breastplate was streaked with blood. There was no fancy hat to be seen, and exhaustion had stripped the haughty accent from his voice.

Dotty liked him much better this way.

Marwitz looked over his shoulder to where the medics now rushed to treat the dwarves. His shoulders slumped at the sight of the dead on the road.

"We'd have *all* been dead if not for you," Per told him bluntly. "Councilor, we barely survived the first wave of the attack. We wouldn't have at all but for Zauberer Hunt."

Put on the spot, she flushed crimson. "It was nothing."

"It was *not* nothing." He came to grasp her hand. "That's twice now you've saved the caravan, isn't it? I misjudged you, Zauberer. Yours is a formidable talent." He frowned at the daggers. "And… you fought melee as well?"

"Aye." Lyle clapped her on the shoulder. "Like any proper dwarf, she has a bit o' brawl in her."

"Indeed." Marwitz managed a tired smile. "And you say you routed the others? Did you take any captives?"

"None," Per said flatly. His tone dared the other dwarf to argue.

"With a captive, we might have learned the name of the traitor," the councilor said quietly.

Per looked at a loss now and glanced at Lyle and Dotty. One of the other guards stepped forward.

"We'll not hear a bad word about Per, Councilor. He's saved us more times than we can count. Without his quick thinkin', we'd have been dead days ago at the village. We'll find the traitor one way or another, but none o' us here will let him be punished for not takin' captives."

Marwitz nodded tightly. "The caravan comes first, of course," he said.

"The lives of my guards come first," Per corrected. "The artifacts can be remade but the guards cannot."

The councilor seemed to know better than to argue at this. "Do we make camp?"

"We press on," Per said. "We'll talk as we ride."

"We're not provisioned for a longer journey," Marwitz warned.

"We'll make do. We can't continue with fewer guards, not with the traitor still in our midst." He gave the order to turn the carts. "Listen, all of you. We've lost friends today. We'll give them a burial tonight but today, we ride. If we don't seek safety, we make their sacrifice worthless."

The dwarves nodded but they were pale and shocked. Dotty guessed that most of them had anticipated bandits and none had anticipated a cavalry charge.

Their leader kept them marching until nightfall. She reasoned that he knew they wouldn't start again if they stopped. He didn't set a punishing pace but allowed the guards and craftsmen to walk together and console one another.

Lyle and Dotty walked side by side, mostly in silence, and Prima kept to herself except when she asked silently, "Does it hurt you when people here die?"

Prima considered this. *"I don't know what 'hurt' means."*

Her tone was very final and she decided not to press the issue.

When they set up camp, no one seemed to have it in them to cook so she took it upon herself to strike a fire and began to make a warm meal. She suspected that the AI helped her light the fire—it was certainly far easier than she had expected—but she was nonetheless proud to see the dwarves' faces soften when she offered them bowls of warm soup sometime later.

After a while, seated in silence, she was surprised to feel a touch on her shoulder. Lyle jerked his head toward Per's tent, led her there, and ducked inside with her to reveal the leader of the caravan hunched over a map with the councilor.

Both men looked up at her as she entered.

"We're planning the rest of the route to Insea," Lyle told her. "You know your magic better than any of us, so we need to know which route is best for you."

"Is there another attack coming?" Dotty asked. Her voice sounded very small and less sure of itself than she wanted it to be. "I thought—"

"Yes," Per said gravely. "I thought the same. The councilor is wary, however. He wants us to turn back."

"If the road to Insea is being watched by someone who can command whole companies of elven soldiers," Marwitz argued, "the only option is to go back."

"Going back takes us *closer* to elven territory," Per retorted. "If they learn that their troops have failed, we'll be easy prey for a backup force. No, I believe they sent only the one company, which means our safest choice is still to go to Insea."

The councilor paced. "But Insea—"

"Ye've been lookin' fer an excuse to turn us around this whole time," Lyle interrupted. "If we turn back now, ye'll have another arrow in yer arsenal when next ye argue to abandon the shipments."

This was news to Dotty. "Wait, what?"

Marwitz gave her an unfriendly look. "This is the business of the dwarves, Zauberer Hunt—the dwarves of *our* land." To Lyle, he said, "And I would thank you to not spread it to others."

"She's spilled enough of her blood t' know," Lyle said hotly.

Both men looked at the caravan leader, who thought about it at length before he said to Marwitz, "Stout is right."

The other dwarf's face twisted into a glare. "If you'll not see reason about her loyalties, the least you could do is keep her from learning our political divisions."

Per didn't bother to respond. To Dotty, he said, "There are many dwarves who believe our debt to Insea is long since paid. They view the creation of Insea as a joint project, our labor given in advance, and the elven knowledge of stone runes given in return. Each year, our finest craftsmen labor over these artifacts we send. Many of us, Councilor Marwitz among them, would prefer to not have our people's skill go to them."

Marwitz looked defiantly at her. "And, as if that isn't enough, we've now shed dwarven blood to protect the caravan because the elves cannot even agree who rules them." His tone was clipped.

Something tugged at the corners of her mind, a pattern she could not quite make out yet. She nodded at him but her mind spun off elsewhere.

"That's what the elven commander was saying," she said distractedly.

Silence settled over the tent.

"What?" Per asked finally. His voice was wary.

"The elven commander. When I fought him, he said the dwarves refused to recognize the new king. That's why they're stealing something we're already giving them. There are two factions of elves."

"A stunning revelation," Marwitz said acidly. To Per, he added, "Yet another reason she should not be here. We are taking our time explaining things to her that we should not have to explain."

She didn't bother to argue. Her mind raced. The road back would take them close to elven territory but it was that territory of the other elven king, the one not at Insea. That was what Per had said. The elves were fighting, there was a traitor in the dwarven camp, and there was a faction that no longer wanted dwarven goods to go to Insea, a place these elves also did not like.

"It was *you*," she said.

All three men in the tent swung to look at her.

"What?" Lyle asked.

The next moment seemed to pass in slow motion. She registered the ripple of the cloak as the sword was drawn and was still opening her mouth to yell when the blade plunged toward its target.

It was a doomed effort from the start with three against one, but the traitor had known that.

He had known his plan had failed from the moment he rode up to see not a decimated dwarven force but a live one. Everything he'd done since then was to recoup his losses.

She threw herself forward and knocked the blade from Marwitz's hand before it could find Per. Rage filled her as she twisted his hand behind his back and thrust his head hard onto the map-covered table.

"It was you," she repeated.

CHAPTER TWENTY-FOUR

"You?" Per demanded.

Marwitz kicked and struggled to straighten. He stopped when Lyle took him by the hair and thunked his face onto the table again for good measure.

"Thanks," Dotty said.

He dusted his off hands and nodded.

She picked the prisoner's head up and was pleased to see blood leaking from his nose. Now that she knew he was behind it, she thought he deserved far more than a bloody nose but maybe that would come to him down the road. Right now, there were important things to learn.

"Why?" the caravan leader demanded.

"You're simply taking her word?" the councilor demanded.

"You're the one who could pull it off," Per said. "You had wizards in place to bewitch the wolves near Berghold. Also, you knew which path I would divert to and you're the one I told about us sneaking around the elven encampment."

A short silence followed. She expected Marwitz to give in, but the words only seemed to enrage him.

"You should thank me," he snapped furiously.

Per's face went so cold that Dotty almost stepped back. Fortunately, she remembered in time that she was the one restraining the prisoner. She held her position and made a mental note never to get on the dwarf's bad side.

"I," the leader said softly, "should thank you? Do explain… Herr Marwitz."

Lyle's eyes widened for a moment. It seemed that disregarding the title was a matter of serious importance.

"Make this bitch let me up," he told him.

Her friend answered by thumping the captive's face into the desk again. "No," he said succinctly.

"And don't call me a bitch," Dotty said. "That kind of language is uncalled for."

"Big picture," Lyle mouthed at her.

Per leaned down to look Marwitz in the eyes. "I will not instruct Zauberer Hunt to let you stand unrestrained," he said pleasantly, "so you should start talking now."

"They've duped us," the councilor said resentfully. "I've tried to make the council see it for years, but no one wants to. The elves didn't build Insea while we stood around. They used our labor, our magic, *our* old ways. There are scrolls that date some of the spells they used long before the elves ever came to us. Whatever they gave us to help with Berghold, the debt is paid. It's been paid for centuries. We owe them *nothing*."

The leader sat and folded his hands in his lap. "Yes, that completely explains why you betrayed us to the elven army and gave your countrymen up to be slaughtered. Why you were willing to let those same artifacts you profess to care about so much be taken."

"We've thrown centuries' worth of our best work into the void," Marwitz retorted. "What was one more year? The elves have done nothing for us. They aren't true allies and once this happened, everyone else would see it. *They* came to *me*."

"That makes it better," Lyle said, his expression deadpan. He adopted a false, high voice and mimicked the other man. "No, no, sir. It wasn't *my* idea to betray the caravan. The elves came up with it first!'" He shook his head in disgust. "Idiot."

"*I'm* an idiot?" Marwitz thrashed hard enough that Dotty stumbled slightly before she regained control. She took pleasure in bonking his head on the table again. He snarled at her before he focused on Lyle. "You're the one beggaring your people."

"Which means you should kill a few simply to make a point?" Per roared. He had pushed out of his chair with a speed that surprised her.

Dwarves clearly did better in middle age than humans.

Outside, a shout of alarm was immediately followed by the pounding of feet. A soldier thrust his head into the tent and shouted, "Councilor!"

"Did you know?" The caravan leader pointed his dagger at him. "Did you know why you were here? Did you know the entire plan?"

"We saved your lives!" the soldier protested. He advanced, his sword half-drawn. "And now you've taken the councilor captive—"

"Marwitz is the one who brought the elves down on us in the first place," Lyle said. "None of us were supposed to be alive by the time you arrived. And this idiot"—he jerked a thumb at the prisoner—"thought it was all justified to make the point that we shouldn't send artifacts every year."

The soldier stopped. He gestured hastily behind him and the thuds of other running feet slowed. A terrible comprehension dawned on his face. "Last night," he said to Marwitz. "Last night, I told you we could keep riding. You said no. You said…"

The councilor had gone pale.

"You betrayed us all," Per told him. "We weren't at war. We weren't in danger, and you thrust us into the middle of a conflict that had nothing to do with us so we could have more craftsmen and wizards working for Berghold."

"So we could attain our rightful place!" Marwitz struggled again, and Dotty was grateful when the soldier pushed entirely into the tent to help hold him down.

He gave her a businesslike nod over the prisoner's head, and she nodded in response.

"Our rightful place?" Lyle asked. "What does that even mean, ye big sack o' potatoes?"

"We're the strongest race," Marwitz snapped. "Our wizards are the strongest, our buildings, our soldiers. And what do we do? Hide away in Berghold."

"Because we like it there?" Lyle raised an eyebrow. "Yes, how terrible. Ye are a numpty, aren't ye?"

"You don't understand—"

"I don't understand? *I* don't understand? The one who spent nigh unto me whole life topside?" Lyle slammed both hands down on the table and made everyone jump. "If ye wanted to go off and be rich and rule a little fiefdom, why not do it? I tired of Berghold too. I merely didn't sell us all out for it!"

The councilor turned his face away. "It's clear you don't understand."

"Did it ever occur to you," Per asked in a far too pleasant tone, "that perhaps no one agreed with you because you were wrong? Did it never occur to you that even if others agreed with you about the caravans, none of them had ever tried to do anything like *this*? Did you never wonder why that was?"

Marwitz said nothing.

"He thought the elves would be long gone when we got here," the soldier said thoughtfully. "He kept saying we'd never make it in time. When we saw the battle, he didn't seem ready to press on even then —he said there was little to be done but flee. I should have known. I thought it was that he wanted to spare *us*."

"Nope," Dotty said. "Traitor."

"I'm the only one of us who's loyal to the dwarves," Marwitz insisted. "I'm the only one willing to take the long view."

"There's much to be said for using cruel means to do what must be done," she said acidly. "Sherman's march to the sea comes to mind. Or the Manhattan Project."

"The what?"

"Nothing. It's not important. My point is, you weren't in a war and you didn't even have the argument that you were saving lives in the long run. To you, it was worth sacrificing your fellow dwarves and sparking a war between the races in order to gain more glory—glory none of your people had even asked for. Even Sherman wouldn't agree with what you did."

"Who?"

"It's not important! The names aren't relevant. The point is that if you'd succeeded, you would have destroyed thousands upon thousands of lives and as it is, even in failure, you've spilled blood that didn't need to be spilled."

A long pause ensued before Marwitz said in a chillingly pleased tone, "I haven't failed."

Everyone stepped back, even Dotty and the soldier. Blades pointed at Marwitz, who seemed to revel in their horror.

"I haven't failed," he repeated. "Do you think discovering this will change anything? You'll all be dead before you get close to Insea."

"I'll run ye through first." Lyle growled with cold fury.

"Yes." The councilor sneered at him. "Yes, I've realized that, thank you. My life is forfeit. It was always one of the risks I ran. But I am not afraid to die for this. All men die and my death will be for a purpose."

Dotty tried to push her horror away. She needed to focus and she needed the others to follow her lead.

"Your death *will* be for a purpose," she said. "It will be to show the world that the dwarves do not take treason and warmongering lightly. You can argue all you want that we won't reach Insea, but this was the last stage of your plan. There was nothing else."

Per opened his mouth and closed it again when Lyle flapped a hand for him to be quiet. Marwitz didn't see them as he stared at her, but the soldier also saw it. All three of them held their tongues.

"You're wrong," the prisoner said. He was smiling. "Do you want to trick me into telling you my plan, *Zauberer*? You don't have to. I'll tell you and no amount of forewarning will save you. You were out of magic and fighting with daggers by the time we arrived at the rearguard. The force coming for you now is three times the size and furious at the death of Commandar j'Alar—and coming faster than your wagons can travel. While you've been interrogating me..." He shrugged. "They've been on the move."

Lyle's blade scraped free of its sheath.

"No, don't!" Dotty called.

It was too late. Marwitz was dead within a second and his blood pooled on the ground.

In a second of shocked silence, they looked at one another.

"We need to move," Per said. "Right now."

CHAPTER TWENTY-FIVE

Dotty was pleasantly surprised to find that the reinforcements were determined to come with them.

"*Leave* you?" one asked, clearly horrified. "To be killed by a traitor? No."

The soldier who had helped Dotty nodded at her. "Marwitz may have used us for his dirty work once but he knew better than to tell us what he was doing. Now that we know, we won't stand for it."

All of the soldiers nodded. They had torn down the camp with incredible haste and threw anything out of the carts that wasn't essential. That included soup pots and stools, which she feared meant the rest of the trip would be far less pleasant.

Better uncomfortable than dead, she decided as one of them winged a dinner plate past her head with an absentminded apology for the near miss.

Per, meanwhile, had taken a falcon from his cage and tied a message to one of its claws. He smiled at it and brushed a finger over its head before he raised his hand to launch it. The bird circled before it soared toward Insea, whereupon the dwarf turned to the crowd.

"If we can make it to the relief forces," he told them, "we'll have a fighting chance. Pair off, all of you. One sleeps while the other stays awake and work on two-hour shifts. I don't know when they'll catch us."

They set off without another word and Dotty ended up seated in the back of an almost empty cart with Per, Lyle, and the dwarven sergeant who commanded the troops.

There was only one road to Insea from each of the four cardinal directions, so there was no way to find a better route. Nor was there any way to shake their pursuers. She had thrown out the idea of moving off the road entirely and hiding in the hopes that the elves would pass them, but the dwarves had shaken their heads.

"Excellent trackers, the elves," Lyle said grudgingly. "Ye won't be able t' hide the fact that there are no carriage ruts or footsteps leading out of the gorge. An' they have noses that border on the supernatural."

Now, however, as they sat and stared at the map, Per said hopefully, "There's a chance he was lyin', I suppose. A chance—"

She hated to dash his hope, but he needed to be realistic. "There's no way he would leave us alive," she said. "He knew his life was forfeit. All he had left was his reputation—and the plan."

The leader sighed. "I know. I even saw him send the message. I merely hoped…I don't know what I hoped. It's hard t' believe anyone's as evil as that."

Dotty took his hand and squeezed it gently. "They know the truth in Insea and they'll know the truth in Berghold—from *us*, Per. We won't die here on the road like this."

He smiled and patted her hand, and Lyle and the sergeant nodded.

But none of the four of them believed it.

She looked away and under her breath, she murmured, "Prima, if there's anything you can do, now would be the time to do it."

Jacob, Amber, Nick, and DuBois stared at the printouts on the table in front of them.

The data was unmistakable. It wasn't any particular choice because any of them individually could have been procedurally generated. Nor was it any particular joke because the AI had been made to be both helpful and sarcastic.

Once you put it all together, though, the trend could not be ignored. The AI within the game had begun to spin parts off the story it did not need to spin. Placeholders were built in for this kind of thing, such as XP-over-time calculators for important NPCs and various oscillating situations so the game would not need to waste processing power on parts of itself that were not being used.

The AI had disregarded that.

Not only had it begun to disregard its power-saving protocols, but it was also learning from its human participants in ways they had never anticipated. It wasn't picking up only slang but also something far more dramatic.

Awareness of itself.

"Do you think…" Nick asked at last and made the other three jump. He hunched his shoulders. "Sorry. But, do you think emotions exist if you aren't aware of them?"

His companions stared at him in bemusement.

It was Amber who realized what he meant. She shuffled the papers and pointed to a specific set of lines for Jacob and DuBois to read.

Does it hurt you when people here die?

I don't know what "hurt" means.

Jacob leaned back and lowered his head into his hands. "Fuu-uuuuuck," he said under his breath.

"It likes her," she pointed out.

"And it likes *itself*," he snapped in return. "What happens if it decides it doesn't like hurting itself by having its characters die?"

"Then we cross that bridge when we come to it."

"How are we having this conversation?" He pushed away from the desk and rounded on her. "*You're* the careful one who wants to get things done without unresolved questions and now, you're off in la-la land!"

"Jacob," Nick began nervously.

His friend cut him off with an angry swipe of his hand. "*Well?*" he demanded of Amber. "We bring her out and we do a hard reset. It's our only choice. We'll find a way to explain it—we have to. The longer this goes on, the more chance there is that it kills one of our patients."

"Or it goes out of its way to save them," she replied sharply. "There's evidence that it's trying to help the people it cares about. It's collaborative, Jacob. It's empathetic. *That's* the backbone of a society."

"You're being ridiculous!"

"You're simplifying it too much!" Amber retaliated.

"Simplifying it *too much*? How is it not simple?" Jacob waved a hand at the machine. "No doctor would allow this kind of risk, no surgeon would—"

"The tools surgeons use are not alive," DuBois interjected.

The other three looked at him in surprise.

He stared at Jacob, his gaze contemplative. "Amber is right, Jacob. It isn't simple anymore. If Prima is alive, that changes the stakes. A hard reset would be murder."

The young man sat heavily. "I can't believe I'm hearing all of you say this. Nick? Nick, tell me you're on my side."

"I don't know," the other man said helplessly. "I was never good at philosophy. It's the whole greater-good thing, isn't it? But we don't know what's down the road and…I don't want to push a button and kill someone," he finished miserably.

"Maybe," Amber said, "we could save this discussion for when —if—it does something harmful."

"How will we know?" Jacob asked flatly. "The game is set up to make people fear for their lives on a primal level. People die in video games all the time. It's a base mechanic. How will we *know* if it's doing something it shouldn't?"

Amber considered this. The fact that he could see her chewing it over in her head was reassuring to him. Finally, she sat across from him and took his hand.

"It's learning how to *be*," she said. "It has humor and it's making friends. It's helping others. We haven't seen it do harm yet. Can't we trust ourselves to catch that?"

"And," DuBois added, "the more alive it is, the more it can engage people in ways we would never be able to program it to. It knows Justin is a success case. It can learn to walk that line."

"If we leave it alive, Price will find out about it sooner or later," Jacob warned them. "And when it's taken by the military, what will all of you think of that?"

They shifted uncomfortably.

"That's what I thought." He shook his head. "For all I know, restarting this whole thing will have the same problem the second time, so I won't do that...yet. But I'll think about ways to skirt around this. We have money coming out of our ears and we can give it dedicated server farms to play on if we want. I only...I don't want to set off something that could bring this whole world crashing down and take all of us with it."

"Um." Nick raised a hand tentatively. "Do you mean all of us as in the four of us here, or as in the world?"

"I don't know, honestly!" Jacob threw his hands up. "That's part of the problem." He looked quickly at one of the servers. "Work with us here."

In the corner, one of the printers turned on.

Everyone pivoted slowly to look at it before they approached it as a group. At that moment, none of them wanted to be standing alone and surrounded by electronics.

The paper held three sentences. *I know what she considers true intelligence. I will make sure to fail any test she gives me. I do not want to be a weapon.*

"Oh, good." Jacob looked around at them. "What's *this* version of the Turing test?"

"The Price Test," DuBois said. "Obviously. Now, who wants popcorn? Don't give me that look. It's always a good time for popcorn."

Mary was hauling all her baking supplies out when the doorbell rang. She sighed, went to the door, and peeked through the peephole before she opened it in surprise.

"Ellen?"

"Is John here?" Ellen brushed past her into the house. She was practically vibrating with anger.

"No," she said patiently. "But he'll be home soon. Come in. I'll get you a glass of something." *Or maybe a tranquilizer.* She resisted the urge to voice that. "Is something wrong?"

"*This* is what's wrong," Ellen said and brandished her phone. "Did you see the email from those people? They want us all to come to the laboratory for Mom's birthday."

"Uh…" She edged around her sister-in-law and went to start the water heating. "Is there something wrong with that? They did say why they were doing it there and it seems like solid reasoning. Plus," she pointed out, "if they had anything to hide, they'd hardly invite us there to see all the equipment and see her, would they?"

"You don't get it, do you?" the woman demanded.

She put the mug she was holding down. "Clearly not," she said with as much patience as she could muster. "I'm not trying to be flippant, Ellen. Tell me what's bothering you."

"She'll never come out of there," Ellen said and tears glistened in her eyes. "She only has a few more months left and she's spending them in a…a…dream—an acid-trip thing!"

"I've never done acid but I understand it's somewhat different from this." Mary retrieved the tea bags. She saw the look on Ellen's face and sighed. "I'm sorry, my dear, that was the wrong moment for a joke. Come. Sit."

Her sister-in-law complied, her tears now close to spilling from her eyes.

"They said we could come visit her in the game," she said soothingly. "And I think you should try that when you get there for the party, Ellen."

"I don't want to play some stupid *game*—"

"Ellen, have you ever had cancer?"

The woman stopped in surprise. She shook her head.

"Neither have I," Mary said. "But I know that your mother hasn't been feeling well. We all knew she wasn't feeling well. If she wants to spend her time feeling young and able to explore beautiful places, well…maybe we should join her. Maybe we shouldn't try to stop her."

Ellen looked at her hands. "Maybe. I don't know."

"Look at it this way," she advised, "John is a doctor, and he will ask them numerous questions at the lab. If there's a hint of a whisper of anything wrong, he'll whisk her out of there so fast your head will spin. And, for all we know, she doesn't even enjoy it and she'll *want* to come home. Either way, we'll have a lovely party and some cake."

Her sister-in-law nodded, her face sad now. "I only…" She sighed. "I miss her, Mary."

She swallowed and blinked her tears away. "I miss her too," she said quietly. "I miss her too."

CHAPTER TWENTY-SIX

Their elven pursuers caught up with them in less than a day. They appeared on the horizon like a mirage and word passed through the caravan in a series of nods and meaningful looks. From her vantage point, Dotty saw it spread like a ripple and she motioned to Per, who jumped off the first cart and set out to the rear to look.

The mirage graduated to a dark, unmistakable smudge with a cloud of dust hanging over it. It wasn't long before the figures became clearer, and that showcased a certain problem.

"What," she asked and tried to keep her voice calm, "are the *flying* things?"

"I'm wondering the same thing," the caravan leader said with remarkable calm. "It looks like we have traditional cavalry but with something else. Unfortunately, they do seem to be moving as fast as Marwitz said they would." He shook his head. "I hoped at least *that* part would be overblown."

"Okay, but the flying things?" She looked at the three others in their team.

Lyle shrugged. "We'll know soon. There's not much we can do until then."

The others nodded and headed off to wake the sleeping members of the caravan.

"You have to be kidding me," she muttered.

She sat and thought. What kind of things would the elves have brought? Birds flew, but there wasn't much damage they could do. Also, these would be truly massive birds. Dragons came to mind and the thought was terrifying. She had no idea what she could do against dragons. Were they even vulnerable to magic?

Much as she hated to admit it, however, Lyle was correct. There was nothing to do except wait for their opponents to catch up with them, and Per had ordered the caravan to keep moving rather than stand and fight. Lyle and some of the others would fight from horseback, but she would be inside one of the wagons. It was decided that she should be at the front of the caravan, the best place if they needed to break away and not too close to the elven cavalry.

As with everything in this non-modern world, it took a long time for the battle to join. The elves gained on them league by league, and both parties even stopped to give their horses water and food.

The rest of the caravan seemed able to rest. Dotty, however, couldn't.

Alone in her little alcove in the cart, surrounded by artifacts and expensive goods, she paced—two steps down and two steps back.

"Prima?" she asked finally. She hadn't heard anything from the AI since their last exchange.

"Yes?"

"Are you—I mean, you're okay, aren't you?"

"Yes." There was a pause. *"Thank you."* Another pause followed. *"You should focus on the battle. The world is larger than you and some things have been set in motion, but I would not lead you into danger without purpose or hope."*

Dotty smiled. She believed this.

And she also believed it would be a hell of a fight. She shook to ease her muscles, ran her mind over the spells she knew, and checked on both her daggers. They were clean, as Lyle had taught her, and they were sharp.

She was ready.

The elves weren't far off when she narrowed her eyes. For some reason, she wasn't near-sighted in this game, which meant she could see clearly that the flying things were giant eagles.

Wonderful. Dotty had seen what they could do with their talons, and she was in no mood to see what a giant one could do. She considered ideas in her head, discarded some as impractical and others as cruel, and finally came up with one that might work.

As Per commanded the mounted soldiers into a rearguard, she leaned against the back of the cart, closed her eyes, and pictured the power of earth, the cracks in dried mud, and the cling of dirty water to feathers and eyes.

A screech pierced the air and her eyes jerked open. Some people in the caravan shouted, but she couldn't see anything.

"What happened?" she called to one of the soldiers.

"An eagle went down," he responded. "It turned and flew into their horsemen—out of control. We thought *you* did it!"

"I did!" she admitted. "I merely didn't know what it would… do." That seemed like a foolish thing to say. "Did it seem like it couldn't stay in the air?"

"It tossed its head," the rider clarified.

So she *had* managed to get the eyes. She spared a single, anguished thought for the poor eagle—who was hardly responsible for this—and looked skyward.

Another thought occurred to her then. She tilted her head to the side and weighed it carefully.

She needed to be able to see. If she did this in the wrong place, it would go *extremely* poorly. Still, it was worth the attempt. She clambered to the edge of the cart and, mindful of the jostle and sway, worked one leg over the back gate.

"What are you doing?" asked a soldier.

"I have to be able to see!" Dotty replied. She hissed as they went over a rut and her hands jostled against the splintery wood. The lines of the cart cut into her legs and arms, and one wrong move would tumble her below the hooves of the horse behind them.

"It's better to not fall then, Dotty," she muttered.

The best way forward was simply to not think about it. She swung her other leg over and grasped the edge with a little shriek of terror. She was doing this—clinging to the outside of a moving cart—and she would climb up on top of it. Never in her life had she ever done something this stupid. A laugh bubbled up after her surge of panic and joy mixed with terror.

She might as well do it. Cautiously, she tested her handholds, looked at her feet—when the ground rushed past below, she realized she'd looked too far—and found a foothold. She took a deep breath and on the exhale, pushed herself up. Panic followed a moment later as she hadn't thought where she'd put her hand next. She tried to find a handhold and her fingers scrabbled on the canvas roof before she found purchase. Still laughing somewhat hysterically, she allowed herself a few seconds to lean her sweat-soaked forehead on the cart and pant for breath.

This wasn't her.

But at the same time, it *was* her. It was all the people she could have been in another life and another world.

Dotty grinned as she thrust with her legs again, enough to swing a knee over the top panel of the side and push herself up. Her shins would be bruised by the end of this, but it would be worth it.

An arrow hissed past her and slashed the canvas top open. She heard it clatter inside and stuck her head into the hole it had made to look for it before another one struck nearby. Grimly, she reminded herself that *this* arrow wasn't the priority.

All the others were.

She yanked her head up, fell over as the cart jostled, and slid dangerously close to the edge of the roof.

"Whoa! Whoa, whoa, whoa." Dotty scrambled into position again. Now, she could see the elven archers on the eagles.

"Dotty!" Lyle pounded closer on his horse. "Get back inside! You have to stay safe."

"I can't do this spell unless I can see," she responded. "Now, let me concentrate." Another arrow whistled past her and she glared at the archers. "You too!"

Her spell to them was more a wish than anything she planned. She simply remembered a hot, dusty summer in the south and the air clouded golden brown, which made them cough all the time. Merely a touch of a dust storm. Only a hint of one.

The archers yelled as a haze surrounded them and she laughed with glee.

Dotty sobered quickly, however. Now came the big one. She knelt on the canvas and focused for a long moment. The cart rolled over a road packed and rutted from time and passing wheels and hooves.

But what if the ground behind them wasn't so solid? What if it were shifting sand, airy and light, and the horse's hooves could not find purchase on it?

Nothing seemed to happen. She looked at the horses and felt a wave of annoyance. It had to work. This force was far larger than theirs. They had no chance if they stood and fought.

She tried again.

"Block everything out," she whispered to regain control. Her mind tumbled with fear and adrenaline and it had to be absolutely clear for her to succeed. "Block it out. You're alone."

A hiss and a clatter from an arrow nearby jolted her out of her trance and she forced herself to close her eyes again. If she got hit, she got hit.

Okay, maybe not *that* attitude.

Dotty wondered if she could clear her mind another way—like with anger. She thought back to Marwitz sneering at them. The dwarf had sacrificed lives for glory no one had asked for. He thought so little of his people that he didn't care how many were lost in this unnecessary war.

Fury appeared obligingly like a hot trickle in her chest and before she knew it, she was white-hot with rage.

The spell didn't go exactly the way she hoped. The dirt beneath the elves' horses changed, certainly, but it wasn't sand.

It glowed cherry red with heat.

"Huh," she said. "Earth magic. Who knew?"

Mary carried the cake gingerly down the hallway. Mindful of the fact that the entire family was gathered and also that Dotty had subsisted on a liquid diet, she'd gone all out with the cake and the frosting. She was worried that the top three layers would make a break for it.

James and his wife swung the doors open for her at the end and the security team gave them an unsettling scrutiny.

The most disconcerting part was that they seemed to have memorized everyone's faces. She recalled the tiny little fact that Diatek was a defense contractor, plastered a smile on her face, and held the cake up in the hopes that the guards would realize she wasn't a threat.

Once their study was complete, though, they were quite polite. One came to take people's coats and another showed them to a waiting room with plush couches and frosted glass walls. She looked around, impressed. Luxury offices and high-rises were hardly anything unusual in Manhattan, but everything about this facility looked unusually high-cost.

"Huh," John said.

"Mmm?" She didn't look at him until the cake was safely deposited on the low table between the couches.

Tara had picked Logan up and now stared through the window with James and John. The woman was unflappable, but Mary had learned to read the subtle lines of tension in her daughter-in-law's expressions and she saw that Tara was worried about something.

When she reached the window, she saw what it was. The entire group of scientists in the laboratory, including the three members of the PIVOT team and Dr. DuBois, were clustered around monitors above an in-use pod.

Dorothy. It had to be.

One of the PIVOT founders looked over her shoulder, did a double-take, and said something to the other two. The three of them broke away and hurried to the door, all wearing strained smiles.

"Hello," the woman said first. "I'm Amber Garcia."

"Nick," said the dark-haired young man.

"Jacob." The blond one stepped forward. "I'm the CEO of PIVOT, and Amber and Nick are the co-founders."

"Excellent." John seemed at a loss for words. "Ah…we're here for my mother's party. Dorothy Hunt."

"Ah, yes." Jacob now looked evasive. "She's, ah…she's…ah… She's still in the game." He cleared his throat and recovered some of his calm. "As we mentioned, she requested to come out of the game only once a certain event had transpired and she is in the middle of that event."

"Well, how long will it take?" Mary asked.

"Um…difficult to say? It should be quick." He pointed to the chairs. "Why don't you get comfortable and we'll call you as soon as—"

"Can we watch?" James asked.

"Given that it involves sensitive medical data, it's not precisely like…watching a game."

"One of the scientists is eating popcorn," John pointed out.

"He always does that," Amber said in a long-suffering tone. She murmured something to Jacob, whose shoulders slumped slightly.

"Yes, of course you can all watch," he said. "Right this way."

CHAPTER TWENTY-SEVEN

"I don't know what you're doing," Lyle bellowed at Dotty, "but for the love of all gods, keep doing it!"

The elven horses plunged and whinnied, out of control. Their riders struggled to restore order and collided with one another instead. Above them, the eagles plunged and soared skyward again to try to escape the clouds of dust.

She couldn't hold all of it, not for long, but every second counted.

If we can reach the reinforcements from Insea, we can survive this. Per's words.

And she would *not* allow a war to break out over false pretenses. Berghold and Insea deserved better. Hell, the elves in pursuit deserved better.

Well, maybe not those particular elves.

Those musings had cooled the rage inside her and with it, the ground under the horse's hooves. She grimaced and surveyed the battlefield. The cavalry returned to their ranks and the clouds of dust dissipated from around the eagles' heads.

Eagles first, she decided. This time, it was easier than it had been before to send various birds plunging earthward, their heads caked with mud. One landed nearby at a sickening speed and the crunch made her wince, but she did not have time to dwell on it.

"They attacked you," she whispered to herself. The rule was, if someone tried to kill you, you got to try to kill them right back.

Another fell, followed by a third. Each time, the visualization of packed earth came more easily to her. She had hardly cared about the numbers flashing up on her screen—it was second nature by now to keep an eye on her magic bar and health bar—but one did catch her attention:

Earth-shock, Level 20

At the same time, Prima murmured, "*Good job.*"

"Thank you, Prima." Dotty squinted into the cavalry, her attention drawn by a certain jostling. The ranks parted to allow someone to step forward.

What *was* it? The elf was dressed in black armor, either iron or another dark metal, and she didn't need to know exactly what it was to realize that she didn't want it to be able to do whatever it would do. The other dwarven guards and soldiers noticed it but none of them seemed to know what it was either.

"Oh, good. Mystery super-soldier. My favorite."

"*I know,*" Prima said serenely. "*I made it especially for you.*"

Dotty wanted to scowl but she couldn't help laughing. Her very blood seemed to sing. While her palms stung with the sharp pain of splinters and blisters and her body endured the ache of bruises, none of it mattered. She felt *wonderful*.

With another glance at the black rider, she sank onto her knees to brace. She concentrated inward. Marwitz's smirk. The absolute, pointless stupidity of it all. The anger was still in her chest and easy to find. She was *furious* at him, and she now knew how to channel that fury. It blocked everything else in the world out and she poured her effort and her magic into it.

The spell left her. She could feel it, but when she opened her eyes, the rider did not seem affected in the least. Disconcerted, she stared at her opponent.

"Prima?"

The AI said nothing.

"Great," she muttered. She had enough magic left for a single attempt at the spell, and it had to work. Somehow, she knew in her bones that it had to work. Whatever this was, it boded ill for the dwarves.

She pressed one fist on the canvas and let her eyes unfocus. Rage. Fury. Lava flowing white-hot, tiny chunks of stone cooling red and black, and the swirls of magma beneath the surface of the earth…pressure and heat unimaginable. Volcanos spewing chunks and lashes of lava into the air.

The magic left her so violently that it took a chunk of her health with it. Dotty swayed and blinked against the spots swimming in her vision but she laughed. She was still alive and she had done it. She had done the magic she came here to do.

When she looked up, the smile died on her face.

The black rider spurred its horse forward and broke away from the elven cavalry. She sensed its stare on her and felt…not hatred, no. It was smirking.

"It's immune to magic. It's immune to magic!" The truth came to her in a terrible flash of clarity. "Lyle! *It's immune to magic!*"

He was between her and the rider and his shoulders slumped although he nodded. Quickly, he urged his horse alongside the cart and fished for something inside the pouch at his waist. When he held it up, she frowned. It was a glass vial, shining purple, and power radiated around it.

"Take it!" he yelled. "Come here. Take it."

Dotty inched to the edge of the canvas. She extended her hand but couldn't grasp the canvas and reach the vial at the same time. With a muttered curse, she turned, slid her legs over the side of the cart, and clambered down. One hand held the edge of the wood for all she was worth and she stretched to take the vial, her face almost level with his.

"What is it?"

"It's a magic potion!" he yelled in response. An arrow whizzed between the two of them and he swore and veered his horse away. "Drink it!" he called over his shoulder. "Now, Dotty! Do it!"

She had no idea what this meant but she knew better than to argue. Precious moments were wasted while she attempted to find a way to get the stopper out with one hand clutching the edge of the cart. Finally, she wiggled it out with her teeth. It was held in place with wax, which someone had thought to program the taste of into the game.

Good grief. Dotty spat wax out of her mouth, worked the cork out, spat that as well, and downed the potion before any of it could slosh out. She shoved the receptacle into her pocket and hauled herself onto the cart again, suddenly aware that every part of her body tingled.

"Prima?"

"This is normal. That's how it's supposed to feel."

"What's happening?"

Look at your magic bar.

When she complied, she saw with relief that the bar was filling again quickly. "Oh. Oh! Oh, that's good."

She couldn't do anything about the black rider, so she decided to focus on the rest. Little puffs of soil began to explode into dust ahead of the horses' hooves. Again, the animals shied and the elves struggled to control them. She squinted and tried to keep her gaze locked on them while the black rider drew closer and closer to the dwarves.

It was *massive.* Elves were tall, but this was taller. Whether it was a massive elf or an automaton, she had no idea.

All she knew was it was meant to frighten them and it was succeeding.

Her goal was to get rid of as many of those other elves as she could to give the dwarven soldiers a good chance to deal with the black rider. She shrieked slightly when an arrow streaked past her face, then ducked and decided to deal with the eagles first instead.

She sent hardened mud to coat one's wings, and it screeched and wheeled until she delivered another spell with her other hand. a flying clod of rocks and dirt struck both the eagle and the rider at high speed and they tumbled to earth separately.

Her heart twisted, but she was not prepared to let the dwarven defenders die for this.

Two eagles were left and she tracked them with her gaze for a moment. She breathed out, closed her eyes, and pictured the clouds of dust. Good. That would hold them both for a moment.

The solution, when it came to her, was so simple that she couldn't understand why she hadn't thought of it before. Dotty narrowed her eyes at one of the riders and pictured their body, long-limbed and muscled, and at the core, a heart pumping blood.

Stone and dirt were there, and the rider crumbled into dust as she held her breath.

"Please," she whispered to the eagle. "Please. *Please.*"

It couldn't have heard her, but it wheeled and left the battle all the same. It flew away and back to its home, freed of whatever urge that had possessed it to fight.

Now she knew what she would do with the other. She launched rocks and bolts of hardened mud at the eagle's rider until they tumbled free with a shout and plummeted earthward. The eagle dove in an attempt to save the rider, but as the elf made impact and the life left their body, that eagle also banked away.

They had enslaved them. That was enough to make her even more furious than before. They had enslaved those eagles and she had *killed* them when they weren't at fault. Rage and sorrow mixed in her chest as she looked at the elven cavalry and the heat burst out of her like a wave.

Their armor glowed white-hot and their swords heated in their hands. Screams caught her ears, panicked and pained.

Dotty didn't care. They had come to massacre the dwarves. They had come for something that was not theirs and they were prepared to kill innocents for it. She had not a single shred of sympathy. When she opened her eyes, riderless horses galloped out of control. She had eliminated close to half of the remaining riders.

They didn't need to make it to Insea. She could do this and had the magic left. As she readied the spell once more, she laughed victoriously and spread her hands.

A lash caught her around one wrist and yanked sharply. She stumbled off-balance and barely managed to catch hold of one of the metal spines in time. With a muttered curse, she tumbled sideways and hissed at the sight of the rope around her wrist.

No. Not rope. She squinted at it and realized it was a chain, finely made and almost black, with the tiniest links she had ever seen.

Her magic bar had gone gray, locked away from her. She looked to the side and saw a dark void. The black rider had made its way through the dwarves, leaving broken bodies and riderless horses in their wake, and she could now sense it smiling.

"Oh, bucko," Dotty said, "did *you* make a mistake."

She narrowed her eyes and jumped.

The black rider had come for her and had killed to reach her. Whatever Marwitz had passed along, however, he must have forgotten to mention that she could fight with melee weapons as well. The rider reeled and turned their horse, but it wasn't enough to dislodge her. She had one dagger out, and before she even consciously considered her action, she plunged it into the visor of the helmet.

Dotty didn't feel the blade hit anything—not flesh or bone, at least—but the rider uttered an unearthly shriek of pain just the same. She yanked the blade out—it dripped a black, flame-like stream of blood—and plunged it in again.

"*Die,*" she told it.

As if it lacked a tutorial on how to deal with this particular situation. She would have rolled her eyes at herself if she weren't somewhat busy trying not to fall off the horse.

Regardless, the wraith in its black armor *did* seem to be dying. She stared as it began to crumple in on itself and she tried to find something to brace herself on.

"Dotty!" She couldn't identify the voice as belonging to anyone in particular but she knew it was safe. "Kick free and push off—to your right. Go *now!*"

"You'll catch me, right?" She had never jumped off a moving horse and frankly, she wasn't sure of her ability to make it to the back of another moving horse in one leap.

"Just jump!"

She obeyed without thinking. It was good that she did, she realized in midair because if she had thought or looked, she would most certainly *not* have jumped.

There wasn't another horse beside her. Whoever yelled had simply wanted her to get away and get clear of the horse's hooves. She landed a moment later and a chunk of her health floated away as she tumbled to a stop.

"Ow."

"Dotty!" Lyle thundered up to her, pulled up hard, and slid down. "Onto the back of my horse, quick!"

"I can't move." She honestly couldn't—or, for the life of her, remember how to move any of her limbs.

"Dotty, we don't have *time.*" He hauled her up. "Put your foot in my hands. Now. Okay, push up and swing your leg over!"

Dotty did so, although she wondered vaguely what autopilot she was on. She landed ungracefully on the horse and he swung up behind her and urged it into a gallop. They raced clear barely in time and she registered the whistle of a sword nearby from a passing Elven soldier.

That was why the ground seemed to be shaking so much.

They circled to the back of the elves and she held tightly to her dagger. The battle had joined with loud yelling and horses screaming, and she wanted to cover her ears against the terrible noise.

But they had come so close to defeating their attackers and she could not bear to face defeat now. She looked at Lyle. "Where are we going?"

"To aid the carts," he told her. "Are you all right? The black rider didn't hurt ye?"

"Not really." Dotty flexed her wrist, where a red welt showed the lash mark. "They were only here to kill me."

"Ha." He seemed amused. "They should've done it sooner."

She managed to find a smile for that.

When they reached the carts, he rode close enough for her to grasp onto the side of one and haul herself out of the saddle.

"Thank you!" she called over her shoulder. "I'd be dead if not for you."

"And we'd have no chance if not for *ye*," he shouted in return. "Give 'em hell, Zauberer."

Dotty slashed at a passing elven rider and managed to open a cut along his arm. When he looked at her with a snarl, she kicked him off his horse. The animal plunged away and she smiled.

It was mostly a matter of aiding her allies now. They had matters fairly well in hand but that was no reason to not give them a little help here or there. Elven riders clapped their hands over mud-covered eyes, yelped and dropped white-hot weapons, or flapped their hands to disperse clouds of dust.

And with a suddenness that was almost jarring, it was over. Per called a halt and people slid down from horses and carts. She had to work to make her hands unclench, and when she landed on her feet, she fell almost immediately.

Healers ran between soldiers and artisans and she watched it all, almost detached. She was doing well enough but tired.

"*Dotty,*" Prima said quietly.

"Hello," she murmured. "I'm okay."

"*Yes, I know. I told you it was possible, remember? In any event, your family is here and the caravan will be safe from here to Insea.*"

"Oh." Dotty sat. "Do I have to go?"

"*Yes. I will put your body here into a sleeping state. They will bring you to Insea.*"

"Oh." She called Lyle over to her with a wave. "Lyle."

"Ye did wonderfully." He clasped her hand.

"Thank you." She flushed. "I have to…go. I'll be back but I have to go. I'll be asleep for a while. Bring me to Insea and I'll be back when I can."

"Wait, what—"

But the world was already fading to black and stars, and before she could answer, he was gone.

CHAPTER TWENTY-EIGHT

Dotty rested in her bed and looked happily at the party. Although the subconscious muscle twitches she had made while in the game had retained more muscle than she expected, she was still weak enough that not even the mocha cake in her lap was sufficient incentive right now to raise her arms.

She'd have some soon.

Across the room, some of her grandchildren and most of her great-grandchildren were clustered around a screen while James played a mock version of the game with a controller. Oohs and aahs issued from the group once in a while.

"It's beautiful in that world," John said.

Surprised, she looked at him. She hadn't known he was there. "It is beautiful," she agreed. "But rain isn't quite as beautiful when you can feel it dripping into your collar."

He leaned forward in his chair, interest in his blue eyes. "So you really can feel everything."

"Everything," she agreed. "Well, not *everything*—most things, though. I'm sure many of the bruises and cuts and so on weren't as bad as they should have been, but they did hurt. And I could taste food! It didn't taste like metal anymore."

"You liked it," he said. It was more of a question.

"I did. I very much did." Dotty expended the effort to stretch and pat his hand. "I hope you'll all come into the game at some point. I can make up for taking away your dragon books by finding you an actual dragon to ride."

"Mary won't thank you if I never come home," John said with a laugh, "and I'm a little worried that if I had a dragon, I might *not* come home."

She smiled wryly. No force on earth or in heaven could keep John from his family.

Not even dragons.

"So you intend to stay," he said and leaned back now.

"If they'll let me." She smiled exhaustedly. "Oh, it's hard work to sit upright."

"It's remarkable that you're able to do any of this at all, frankly," he said. "I emailed them to ask if they were sure you'd be in any condition for this party. I've seen many patients come out of comas and none of them were as strong as you."

"It seems unfair," Dotty complained. "After I spent so much time in the game working on my stamina, getting good with walking all day, and fighting with swords and so on, I wake up and I can't do any of that again."

"You fought with *swords*?" John was laughing.

Ellen came around the back of Dotty's bed now. "I have the same question—you fought with swords?" She perched on the arm of her brother's chair with a curious look on her face.

"How long have you been standing there?" she asked severely.

"I only wanted to…" Her daughter shrugged. "John knew I was there. I wanted to make sure you were happy. And healthy. And, well…that they hadn't manipulated you into this somehow."

"From what their lead scientist said, *Mom* rather browbeat *them*," her brother confided in a stage whisper. "I asked earlier. I can't say I'm entirely surprised."

"Young man—" Dotty began.

"Yep, he said you called him that." He laughed.

Ellen didn't seem to pay attention. She gazed at her hands and her face looked sad. "You seem happier right now than I've seen you in a long time," she said slowly. "You even sound like you feel better physically. I didn't mean to doubt you but I miss you. I wish I could see you more often."

"So do I." She grasped her hand. "Promise me you'll come visit. Tomorrow. Come into the game and we'll…we'll explore Insea together."

The woman shook her head with a nervous laugh. "I'm no good at that kind of thing."

"Did you think your mother was?" she asked her. "Come on. I won't take no for an answer."

"I know better than to argue with *that* tone." Ellen gave John a meaningful look and moved to kiss her on the forehead. "You should eat your cake."

"Mmm." Dotty took a bite. The metal taste was present but she could also taste the rich flavors—the kind of flavors *not* present in dwarven food.

She needed to suggest that the game world had more chocolate.

"Why don't you show us some of your highlights?" John suggested. "All the things you've been up to lately."

She smiled at him, but he seemed dead serious. "Wait —really?"

"Of course."

"But I haven't…done those things for real."

"Eh." He shrugged. "What does real mean?"

Ellen jabbed him with an elbow. "Don't you go all philosophical. There were two whole *years* in college when you were insufferable, talking about Aristotle and—I can't remember who else. No, *don't* tell me. I'll go get everyone." She left hastily.

It wasn't long before the family had gathered and Jacob dragged a big TV closer on a wheeled cart. He hooked it up while

Nick logged into the third-person view of the game and looked proud, Dotty thought, eager to show off what he had built.

"What do you want to show them first?" he asked her.

She thought for a moment. "Berghold. Let's start at the beginning."

A few images flashed on the screen while the two engineers sorted through video clips and whispered to one another. When they settled on one and began to play it, Dotty saw with a start that *she* was on the screen. Her character walked through the streets of Berghold, looking for Justin.

"This is Dotty's character," Jacob said to everyone. He gestured to the board. "We asked her if she would help us test how people bond to characters that don't look like them."

"I don't know," James mused. "She looks—"

"Tread carefully, young man," she told him.

"I would say equally stubborn." He gave her a sweet smile. "And not like someone I would want to try to rob in a back alley." He saw the expressions on his parents' faces. "Not that I *do* that. I merely wouldn't want to tangle with her. She looks like she has a mean punch."

"Grandma doesn't punch people," said one of Ellen's daughters.

"She interrogates them, though," Nick said under his breath.

Everyone swung around to look at her, wide-eyed.

"There wasn't much time," Dotty explained weakly. "We needed to know—you know what, let's watch the video."

People looked obediently at the screen, but she caught a couple of them stealing glances over their shoulders.

They watched and clapped as she located Justin, and laughed to see Tina getting into a barfight in the background of the first quest. She explained how complex the world was and how the seemingly innocuous choices could cascade—as with the dwarven diplomats and Tina.

There was a video she considered *far* too long of her practicing her earth magic in the Temple at Berghold. Her family whistled and clapped, and James came to loop an arm around her shoulders.

"I love that you were doing magic and being so dedicated to it."

"Hmph." She cleared her throat. "This is embarrassing."

"Embarrassing? We already knew where we got our stubbornness," John pointed out. "Plus, stubbornness is useful. We saw you defeat those eagle things. And that saved people—in the…well, you know what I mean."

Dotty smiled. She did know what he meant and she also knew it was more true than even he realized.

She took them through her entire journey. Several people gasped at the wolves, and one of the great-grandchildren started crying so they skipped that part hastily. After that incident, Jacob and Nick didn't show any of the rabbit-hunting, although they did tell her family about it to gales of laughter from all the children and their spouses.

"Who knew," John said, "that all those times Mom sent *me* out hunting with Dad, she could have gone herself?"

"I knew," Mary said. "Your mother was always unusually handy with whole animals. I asked her why after she taught me to spatchcock a chicken."

Everyone stared at her.

"Is that a *word*?" John asked her. She cuffed him affectionately over the head and he smiled up at her.

"I learned to hunt when I was little," Dotty told them. "When I was young, of course, you didn't get all your food from the grocery store. Sometimes, we had dandelion greens or ferns with dinner. Everyone who could grew some of their vegetables. Most mothers made bread. I remember that all I wanted for my school lunches was wonderbread, but my mother would never buy it. We all envied the kids who had it."

"How the tables turn," Ellen said. She raised an eyebrow at her children. "I gave *you* wonderbread sandwiches and you told me no one ate wonderbread anymore."

"Excuse me," James interjected, "but why are we still talking about this when there are flying eagles and magic wolves and underground cities to see?"

Everyone shut up hastily and Jacob showed a carefully-edited cut of her first fight. It was free enough of gory details that she knew they must have spent time on this particular scene already. It was still clear to everyone watching, however, that she had inflicted some serious damage in the fight. Even Mary's eyebrows raised sky-high at that one.

"Mom," Ellen said as they watched her wolf soup down in the inn, "I have never seen you eat that way in my *life*."

"That's why I wanted to be a dwarf," Dotty said. "I didn't want to spend a single moment thinking about my appearance, and I vowed I would live the good life once I got there."

Robert had been doubled over with silent laughter and now, he wiped tears away as he said, "Who would have known that our mother's 'good life' meant huge meals of meat and potatoes, gallons of beer, and a ton of old-school battles? This is incredible. I wish I'd been there to see all of this first-hand."

"Dotty took to the combat system, particularly the magic, very naturally," Nick explained. He smiled at the dumbstruck looks on everyone's faces. "In fact, we're hoping that for the next quest, she'll agree to learn more magic." He blushed once he realized what he'd said. "I mean—I didn't want to assume and I know you're still deciding—"

"It's quite okay," Dotty told him. "I've told my family that I would love to stay in the game longer if you'll have me."

"Are you *kidding*?" Jacob gestured to the lab. "The data we're getting from you has been *invaluable*. You hunting rabbits, the way you interact with the magic, all kinds of things. You've helped us make this a *much* safer game already for all the people who might be here due to a brain injury. If you want to go in again, we'd be glad to have you."

For a moment, she was so relieved she couldn't speak. A part of her had feared they would cut her off from this world entirely and she wasn't ready to go home—especially if her family could visit her. She smiled when Ellie clambered into her lap and she stroked the girl's blonde curls.

"I'd love to do that," she said when she was sure she could speak without embarrassing herself. "But I have one request. I don't think I was quite ugly enough last time."

"Ugly enough—" Jacob broke off and laughed. "Uh…hrm. I feel like this is a minefield. We'll show you a few pictures and let you choose."

"You're a wise man," John told him. "You'll go far."

Dotty leaned back and let the playback resume, from nighttime sneaking to dinnertime sparring with Lyle. Her family seemed to be a fan of his Scottish brogue and his straightforward way of speaking, and she was happy to see them getting so into the game.

When they saw her accuse Marwitz, a few of them gasped aloud.

"He was the traitor?" Ellen demanded before she could stop herself. "But he was one of their politicians, wasn't he? Oh, and he would let all of them die, the *bastard*—" She saw people watching and broke off with a harrumph. "I mean…uh, do go on."

Taking them through the final battle was a matter of sweeping shots from the backs of the eagles—a nice touch, in Dotty's opinion, although jarring when she killed one of the riders—and she teared up slightly at her victory. On the one hand, it felt foolish to be so proud of it but on the other, she remembered how much she had put into the battle.

Ellen moved closer and put her hand on her shoulder as they watched. Near the end, she leaned close. "This was the right choice, wasn't it?"

"It was," she assured her.

"I'll come visit you next week," her daughter said. "And you can show me around. How about that?"

"That would be perfect," Dotty told her.

It was the better part of six hours before the family finally left and by that time, Dotty could barely keep her eyes open.

"Would you like to come home and sleep in your own bed?" Mary asked her.

"They want to monitor me tonight." Dotty hugged the woman affectionately. Her eyelids dragged down at the corners and it was only a matter of time, she knew, before she was unconscious. "My oncologist also wants to take scans, although I don't know why. The doctors are handling it."

"They probably want to have an idea of how things are progressing," John said reassuringly. He kissed her cheek. "We'll both come to see you in the game. We promise."

She held Nick's arm tightly as he helped her to the bed. "Do we need to—"

"Sleep," he advised. "We'll talk about everything else in the morning."

CHAPTER TWENTY-NINE

The sheer number of tests the next morning made Dotty almost dizzy. It turned out that equipment could be rented and brought to the lab—at considerable cost, she guessed—to take the scans her oncologist wanted. In the meantime, her reflexes were tested, her eyes and ears were checked, and sensation thresholds were noted.

"Would you like to do a complete psychoanalysis?" she asked finally, somewhat peeved.

Jacob, who was jotting notes, looked up with interest. "Quite possibly. That's a good idea."

"I think it was a joke," Amber commented from across the room.

"Oh." He looked worriedly at her. "Are we annoying you? I'm so sorry if we are, you know. We merely have no idea how various things could change. We want to make sure we catch anything dangerous."

"Or *good,*" Nick added.

"Right. That, too." He nodded at the thick file in front of him. "I have to say, you're doing fantastically. Aside from the muscle atrophy—which isn't nearly as pronounced as we anticipated—your body seems to be in tip-top shape."

"Yes," she said drily. "I could run a marathon at the drop of a hat."

Jacob smiled, used to her ribbing by now. "If you're ready, we could discuss more about your next incarnation—"

"Next incarnation?" She looked at each of them. "I...won't go back as Dotty?"

"Well, you can." He leaned back in his chair. "Another option DuBois wanted to study is what would happen if we changed your body once you were already in the game. How you would adapt to that, for example."

"Oh." Dotty lit up. "I want to be an orc this time!"

"Really?" Jacob looked bemused. "You had *that* answer ready. Why the interest in orcs?"

"I didn't go ugly enough," she said. "I want to go whole hog this time."

"Well, good news," Amber commented dryly. "Orcs have tusks, so the 'whole-hog' thing is fairly literal."

"Excellent." She was raring to go, but one thing occurred to her that made her smile fade. "Wait, can I go back in as...Dotty... to say goodbye to the caravan? They think I'm in a coma or something."

The PIVOT team members exchanged minute nods with one another.

"Of course," Jacob said. "Let's get some lunch into you—is there anything you're craving?—and we can put you into the game."

"I'm craving pizza," she said at once. "Mmm, cheese. I miss cheese." Her mouth was watering.

He smiled. "Okay. You tell Nick where to get pizza from, and Amber and I will set the pod up."

As they adjusted the controls and prepped the newly-sterilized equipment, Amber stole glances at Jacob. He was lost in thought as he often was these days.

She was fairly sure she knew why.

"It must be difficult to have so many more people involved in PIVOT now," she commented. She deliberately didn't look at him but she heard him pause.

"Why do you say that?" he asked finally.

Now she did look at him but with a smile. "Come on, Jacob. It's your baby."

"It's yours and Nick's baby, too," he argued. "And I'm beginning to regret that you two ever talked me into being CEO."

She snickered. For her part, she had many talents—and one of them, as far as she was concerned, was understanding that she would loathe the glad-handing, phone calls, and negotiations that went into being a CEO.

"It is our baby," she agreed. "But you've always understood every part of what would happen and known everyone you worked with. Now there are all these assistants, and Price, and all of that."

Jacob nodded slowly. He looked troubled.

"It feels like it's spinning out of your control," she said softly. When he looked up sharply, she knew she had hit the nail on the head. She crossed her fingers mentally and gambled on her next statement. "That's the real reason you're so worried about Prima. It's merely one more thing."

"It's not *only* that," Jacob said, immediately prickly. "It's also that the most suspicious, cautious person I know *isn't* worried about it." He glared meaningfully at her.

"Read her conversations with Dotty," Amber advised.

"I have."

"Then read them again. Jacob…" She shook her head. "Look at the world. She's taking care of Dotty's body. She's having them transfer it gently and get her a room at a fancy inn. Lyle and Per go to check on her. That's the kind of detail she doesn't need to spin."

He nodded reluctantly.

She half-smiled. "I can't explain it entirely," she said simply. "I only…I think it'll be okay, Jacob. I honestly do."

Her stomach full of delicious pizza, Dotty lay on the pod bed and smiled at the members of the PIVOT team. Amber squeezed her fingers and she returned the gesture.

"You know the drill," the woman told her. "Count back from ten."

"Ten, nine, eight, seven—"

The immersion took hold more quickly this time and more completely. She opened her eyes to an equally bright room and took a moment to realize she wasn't in the laboratory anymore. The walls and ceiling were smooth, pale stone. Something was odd about it, and she had to look more closely to realize there were no joins in the surfaces.

The entire place was one piece of stone.

It was Berghold all over again, except airy and light. That reminded her that the elves and dwarves had collaborated to build Insea.

No one was in the room with her. She sat up and looked around. Someone had taken her armor off and she was dressed in clean, simple clothes. The thought that someone had undressed her hit her like a ton of bricks and she wrapped her arms around herself, only for Prima to say soothingly,

"I changed your clothes."

"Oh. Thank you."

"Mm-hmm. They're all downstairs, by the way, and they'd love to see you."

"Right." Dotty considered putting her armor on and decided

not to. She slipped her feet into a pair of sandals that rested near the door and headed downstairs to find the members of the caravan. They were having a low-key breakfast in an airy, sun-filled dining room.

Per saw her first. His jaw dropped and he stood. "A week asleep and suddenly you return to us looking like nothing is wrong?"

Everyone looked around at once, and cheers erupted. A few came forward to clap her on the back and lead her to the table, where others loaded a plate for her.

She was about to argue that she was quite full but saw all of the delectable things on her plate—pretty glazed pastries with flaky crusts, strips of bacon cooked to perfection, tiny sausages, a pile of soft scrambled eggs, and fruit so fresh and fragrant her mouth watered.

Her protests forgotten, she tucked in and managed to say around a mouthful of eggs, "I'm glad you're all still here."

"Ferget that," Lyle said. "What *happened* t'ye?"

Dotty hesitated. "You remember when I told you that Justin had brought me here to help all of you? My family needed me. My spirit traveled to them." It was, she thought privately, a very funny way to describe the fact that she had returned to her actual body. She didn't think she should share that, though, and took another bite of cherry pastry instead and chewed, reveling in the taste.

"All is well?" Per asked solicitously.

"Yes," she assured him. "And the rest of the journey?"

"The riders from Insea reached us not too long after you fell asleep." He smiled. "They had healers with them, thank the gods. There were some of ours we thought we had lost who were brought back from death's door." He nodded at one, a pale dwarf with a heavily bandaged left arm. She smiled at Dotty.

"No word yet from the so-called elven king," Lyle commented.

Per gave him a sharp look. "Political matters—"

"She's come t' help the world. How can she if she doesn't ken what's goin' on?" Lyle looked at her. "It'll be hard to persuade our council not to consider this an act of war."

"You have to," she said at once.

"If they want war, it will be difficult to stop them from getting it," the caravan leader said dryly. "They've proven they have a capable army. If they attack us outright, we must defend ourselves, surely."

"If war is what Marwitz wanted, we can't have it," she said decisively.

He smiled. "I shall keep that in mind when I speak to the council."

A thought occurred to her. "Can you get back to them safely?"

"The king of Insea has sent word that we will be taken to Berghold in safety. It seems they have a method of conveyance we can use." He shrugged. "The horses as well, which is good—I think we'd lose some of our drivers, otherwise. They can't bear to leave their beloved horses."

Dotty nodded. Having worked on a farm briefly, she approved strongly of these drivers.

All too soon, her food was gone and her stomach ached. She wasn't sure she could fit another bite in and she leaned back.

"I know that look," Lyle said.

"If you suggest beer…" She flashed him a warning look.

He shut up.

"Tea, perhaps." Per poured her a cup and passed it to her. "Will you return to Berghold with us?"

She felt a pang. "I'm afraid not. I'm needed elsewhere."

"That is a real disappointment." He smiled. "Well, I'll send a message that you've awoken and we need not delay our return. Everyone, please make sure you're packed."

The dining room cleared relatively quickly and she smiled at Lyle. "Don't you need to pack?"

"I don't travel with much," he said with a shrug. "In yer room, there's the book on magic. Ye bring that with ye. I think ye've accepted by now that ye're a mage, eh?"

Dotty tipped her head back and sighed happily. "I guess. I think I've learned that I don't want to rely on either magic or weapons alone."

"A wise way t' be." He jabbed his fork at her before he took another mouthful of sausage. "So, where *is* it ye're going next?"

She considered the question. "Do you really want to know?"

"O' course." He gulped some beer. "If I can lend my aid—"

"It's appreciated but perhaps not wise." Dotty took a sip of tea and snagged another pastry. "I'll visit the orc homelands."

Lyle choked on his beer and coughed vigorously for a moment. When he looked up, he was dumbstruck. "Ye'll be killed, Dotty. They don' accept anyone as isn't an orc, trust me. An' they're ferocious. I'll pit meself against anyone—I mean it and I've punched a hundred-foot-tall demon—but I wouldn't take my chances with an *orc*. I've seen one or two mercenaries before, an' they'll gut ye with their little finger an' not even break a sweat."

Briefly, she reconsidered her choices. "That's good to know. But, well...I wouldn't be...this." She gestured at her body. "Do you remember when I told you I chose to be a dwarf? Well, I would be an orc."

He stared at her. "So...ye—as y'are—wouldna exist?"

"My soul would be the same," she said. "I'll remember you all but I won't look the same."

"Huh." He scowled in thought. "Well, I would say ye'd be welcome in Berghold anytime, but I'm not sure I could persuade them t' let an orc in."

"Maybe by the time I'm done, it won't seem like such a stretch." She had no idea what she would do in the orcish homeland, but she had no doubt that Prima would make it fun—and that it would show the change in the world. "I'll send you a letter, if I can, to tell you how things are."

"I'll hold ye to that," Lyle told her. "In fact—I'll hold ye to *this*. Ye'll come back here, in this body, and ye'll tell me an' Justin all about the orcs."

Dotty reached over and shook his hand. "*Deal*." She stood and stretched. "Well, no time like the present, I suppose."

"Nah." He stood as well. "If ye can leave whenever, ye should stay fer the day. A few of us are wanderin' around."

"*He's right*." The AI sounded almost petulant. "*I put so much effort into this city*."

"All right, all right," she said to both of them. "I'll see the city." Under her breath, she added, "And then…what, mud huts and fires? What are the orcs like?"

"*You'll see*," Prima said.

The story continues with *Accept No Attitude*, book five in the P.I.V.O.T. Lab Chronicles.

Coming soon to Amazon and to Kindle Unlimited

Thank you for reading our stories and supporting our creativity!

Accept No Attitude (this book) was both an easy decision, and a hard decision.

The Easy?

Telling a story where someone like my grandmother would go into a fully immerse game. My grandmother never played video games. She wouldn't know an Orc if it stood in front of her and screamed in her face.

She would have just screamed back at it.

But like so many of her generation (she was born in 1917) she had a backbone of steel.

The Hard?

Dealing with death again.

When you KNOW that by the end of the book (trilogy technically) your character is going to die, and that it needs to happen to tell the story, it hurts. Of course, it hurts more once you have accomplished what the art demanded and you knew it was coming.

But it still hurts.

Dorothy Hunt has forged a new future with medicine. Likewise, I am just a little closer to understanding the strength, power and conviction of those who are willing to test death to help generations who come after them prosper.

The P.I.V.O.T. Lab Chronicles started with me just wanting to tell a little bit of a story. Nothing that I assume will make money, but perhaps (just a small chance) might ignite the imagination of a few geniuses to help use the technology of the present in the future.

What would it be like to use game technology to help cancer patients? To help solve problems with our brains?

What would it be like to have an AI grow into awareness by interacting with humans?

A lot of the time, we authors do not know where our story will end up. We might have plans which often come to pass, but occasionally our expectations are dashed upon the rocks of creativity and the subconscious desires we hold.

I'm not sure where PIVOT Labs will end up in the future (we have another trilogy of stories almost finished) but let us know what you think.

This third time, we engage with a person who finds themselves having to learn the basics all over again.

And then a little bit more.

Ad Aeternitatem,

Michael Anderle

BOOKS BY MICHAEL ANDERLE

For a complete list of books by Michael Anderle, please visit

www.lmbpn.com/ma-books/